Enjoy the Book

Dec 06/2022

Two Stars For A Lost Soul

This work of fiction is dedicated
to Beverley Wilson, whose belief
in Christmas has never wavered.

Prologue

Antonio Barbossa, some would say, was given a raw deal when it came to life. First, a terrible accident when he was young sent him to an orphanage, leaving him alone with no family or friends. Then, after years of hard work, Tony was given a break or a gift, some would say. A series of flashing lights awoke him from a dead sleep in his room at the mining camp he often called home. Tony got up and looked out his window to the east. There, the northern lights were dancing up a storm. Greens, blues, reds, and violet made a series of movements, creating a sky of wonderment. As Tony looked out the window, he saw two stars shining in all their glory and beckoning him to follow their lead. What were they, and why did he see them this morning?

December 1985, Antonio Barbossa, Tony for short, up at 6:00 A.M. It was dark in the North Country. He lay for a minute, thinking about how he got here, then stretched and sat on the edge of the bed, slowly realizing this would be the last day in camp. Got the strength to move from the bed, grabbed his kit, and headed to the shower room.

Many people thought Tony was a loner. He was not; he enjoyed people just as much as the next guy, but the nature of his job gave him a lot of alone time. However, with one qualification, Tony preferred to be by himself at this time of the year. Christmas and birthday memories were not good and have been that way for several years.

Tony was not overly tall, just under 6 feet, weathered, face windburn, and tanned. But he was in great shape as all the hard work tramping around the bush in summer and winter kept him in good condition.
Looking at himself in the mirror, his brown piercing eyes looked back at him, telling a story; his hair, long and curly, didn't look too bad. Still, the scraggly beard must go; the mustache will stay.

Tony jumped into the shower, unsure what the next adventure would be. His 45th birthday was coming up on December 24th, a time for recollection and joy, but this time of year never brought smiles or warmth to his heart. Instead, it was a sad time for Tony.

In 1955, Tony and his parents, Antonio and Maria, were going to the midnight service on Christmas Eve. They were entering the last intersection before the parking lot. Antonio looked to his right. All he could see were the headlights bearing down on them. Antonio hollered. Hang on, they were broadsided. Tony learned that his mom and dad had died instantly. There was no fault; the oncoming vehicle's gas pedal froze. That night, Tony's life changed forever. He was taken to the hospital, unconscious with a nasty cut to the head, badly bruised legs, and a broken arm. He could not remember much except being tossed around like a rag doll, his mom screaming, and his dad yelling, hang on before he fell unconscious. When he came to and was told what had happened, he vowed never to step foot in a church and never celebrate Christmas or his birthday again.

Tony recovered, at least physically. He became a ward of the state, an orphan with no family. He left his hometown of Thundering Waters, traveling to an orphanage in the state's southern part. Moving away from the big lake with ships from around the world visiting. While growing up in the orphanage, Tony spent much of his time studying; he was bound and determined to succeed. He remembered his dad saying, make sure you get an education, my son. It will be the stepping-stone to a better life. Tony completed high school with good marks.

The orphanage's people were firm disciplinarians and ensured education was high on the list; other orphans succeeded while others did not. Tony had no idea what life was going to bring. One of Tony's mentors was interested in the study of rocks. This intrigued him, how a person could make a living looking for different types of stones. He graduated and became a geologist/prospector with a firm understanding of what makes a mine. Since then, he had been tramping all around the countryside, always looking for a pot of gold.

Tony worked for several mining companies in the early years. Then, in 1975, he set out and opened his own company and became his own man. The Eagle Mining and Prospecting Company was born. Over the years, he had set aside a good portion of his earnings for the future. An insurance company finally tracked him down, and he discovered a payout for him from that fateful night in 1955. This also helped with his new venture, providing the necessary capital for him.

In the summer of 1979, Tony was in the North Country on a trip to an area where he had heard some promising rock formations needed to be looked at. This information came from an evening of entertainment in a local drinking establishment. No one paid attention to this information; people just considered where it originated. Tony listened; he had some time on his hands and decided to check it out on the quiet side. Tony spent part of the summer wandering throughout the area. Spending countless hours looking at rocks of every sort, Tony felt it was time to give up on this swamp hole. Time to head back to Dark Lake, as his ride back to Pike Waters would be landing shortly. He was returning to the rendezvous location when he tripped over a fallen tree. He slid into a bog hole; Tony grabbed a handful of moss to keep him from sliding into the hole and getting wet. It was nothing dangerous, but he got wet; the air turned blue with the superlatives from his mouth. He wanted to stay dry. The plane coming to pick him up and fly him back to civilization was circling overhead, getting ready to land. It was going to be a wet ride, Tony thought. Looking at his hand, he was holding a large piece of moss that must have slipped off the rock when Tony reached for a handhold so he wouldn't slip into the water. Tony turned, and a shiny-looking rock outcrop was staring him in the face. There was a vein of something yellow staring back at him. Tony thought, now this is interesting. Got up wet from the waist down, looked closely at the vein, and realized this was it. He got his bearings. Marked the spot on his map and placed the moss back over the outcrop. He did not want any other prospector to happen along and stumble over his discovery. This outcrop could be a sign for the future, or it could be a bust.

Tony hiked back to the edge of Dark Lake. The Cessna was waiting for him; he threw his gear in, climbed into the seat next to the pilot, took off, and headed to the little town of Pike Waters. Smooth 80-minute flight. Looking out the window, he saw nothing but water, forest, and nothing else. A secondary highway, split the landscape like a black snake. Finally, he landed in Pike Waters and got a ride to the motel where he was staying. Before he left, he booked the plane back to Dark Waters in a couple of days.

That night, Tony went to the local establishment to hear news about the area he had just come from. Scuttlebutt said a group of prospectors was staking claims about ten miles west of where he had been. Tony was happy the plane for the return trip had already been booked. But, first, he needed to find help to ensure he could correctly claim the property he wanted.

Before Tony flew to Dark Lake, he met a fellow, Adam Watson. He told Tony to keep him in mind if he ever needed help. Adam was about six and a half feet tall, mid-thirties, with long red hair and a bushy red beard to go with it. Piercing blue eyes, arms like tree trunks, a big man, trim and muscular but always smiling.

Adam was known to have a drink or two, sometimes getting him into trouble. He loved playing cards. The bigger the pot, the better, even though Adam was a terrible player. So Tony figured he might be ready to go to work. Tony looked around and found Adam sitting in the corner, nursing a beer.

Tony walked over to him, "Well, young feller, what are you up to."

"About six foot five and a half, and you, how can I help you, old timer."

"Would you like to go to work for a while? Room and board supplied low wages, a chance to make a million."

"When do we leave."

"The day after tomorrow, we will gather supplies first. Then fly out at 8:00 A.M. the next day."

"Fine, will see you in the morning." With that, Adam finished his beer in one gulp, got up, and left.

Friday morning, Tony met Adam at the seaplane base. Adam was there earlier and had the plane loaded. So they climbed aboard and took off.

Adam then asked, "You going to tell me what we are up to and where we are going."

"We are heading to a small lake called Dark Lake, land there, set up our camp, then we will stake around twenty to thirty claims from a spot I discovered a couple of days ago."

Dark Lake came into view, the water looking blackish from the air. The lake was surrounded by black spruce and bogs everywhere. They found a nice spot and set up camp.

The next day, they started staking claims from the outcrop, where Tony discovered the vein buried below the moss. They got twenty-five claims staked, and then they ran into other prospectors staking land, not that they had found anything, just locking the property up. So, it was good that Tony decided to jump the gun and get his claims staked. After a couple of weeks, they flew back to Pike Waters. Tony went to the Mining Recorders Office and recorded his claims.

Tony and Adam discussed working together and reached a gentleman's agreement. They flew back to Dark Lake and started to work the area to see what would be in their future. They put all their energy into this forbidden swamp hole for the first two years. She did not want to give up her secrets. The tiny vein was the only bright spot.

The following year, Tony made a deal with a geophysics company to do some exploratory work for a small stake in the ownership of the property. It looked like the vein Tony discovered was the only thing showing promise, which wasn't much. The geophysics study started, but no results were forthcoming. The operator could not get results consistent with his observations over the years. Sent all his equipment out to get recalibrated and checked. Money was running out.

Adam decided to cut and run; he had heard about other areas showing distinctive gold signs and wanted a part. Tony bid Adam farewell and realized he would have to break into the private funds he kept for a rainy day. Tony gave Adam some money and sent him on his way. Tony thought that if this property became a winner, he would look Adam up. Wonder where Adam was. Tony had something for him. Now, five years later, he had never heard from Adam. In fact, he had no idea if Adam was still alive.

Tony's property ended up showing promise; the hard work paid off. Two-Jacks Mining Corporation, a new mining company, heard about his property and offered to purchase the claims from Tony. After some due diligence, a lucrative offer was presented. He thought about it for five minutes. Tony would never have to work again. Finally, he decided that the intent to purchase would be signed at 11:00 A.M. today. Tomorrow, Tony will be in Thundering Waters, visiting the Two-Jacks Mining Corporation office, where the final contract will be signed. Then, the funds would be transferred into Tony's account at the Thundering Waters Bank.

The intent to purchase was now signed. It was time to catch the greyhound in Pike Waters and head to Thundering Waters' Tony's hometown. The trip would take at least eight hours. It has been a long time since Tony visited Thundering Waters for any length of time. Thinking about when he left all those years ago, he had a lot of memories, some good and some horrendously bad.

He finally arrived at the Thundering Waters bus depot as the bus traveled from the early morning into the next day. Then, finally, it was time to get off; he gathered his belongings and went to the hotel. He remembered the building like it was yesterday. It was still a spectacular place.

Two Jacks Mining made the arrangements for Tony, so all he had to do was check-in. The front desk looked at him like he was a slug crawling out from under a rock. He paid no attention, went to his room, relaxed, and fell asleep for a while.

When Tony awoke, he decided it was time to shower and change into other clothes. Then, he ventured to Two Jacks Offices and signed the final contract, releasing his interest in the Dark Water venture.

It was time to find a restaurant for a meal, walk downtown, and see what had changed and what was still the same.

After he strolled down the Street looking for a place to eat, he came across Vi's Tavern, looking pretty good from the outside; he thought this could be a great place to eat. Tony walked in and wasn't sure if he would stay dark and dingy, plants all over, English ivy covering the ceiling, windows with years of grime. The only thing missing, Tony thought, was birds; they should be all over squawking, making a racket and a mess. Tony was about to leave when he suddenly heard, "whadda you want, you comin to eat or just drink."

Tony spun around, and there was a little lady with long, greying hair, a cigarette hanging from her mouth, in a dirty white tea shirt with a semi-white apron to match. Tony wanted to run, but it was too late.

"Come in; my name is Vi. I have gnocchi and meatballs; that's, ah, my specialty. Sit down. I bring you order. Whata you want to drink, a glass of a red Chianti, okay done."

Tony just accepted the order, sat down, and waited. Then, finally, the meal came, and it melted in his mouth.

"Whatsa you name?"

"Antonio Barbossa," Tony replied.

"That's a gooda name."

Then, after a few glasses of wine, it was time to go out for a stroll. Tony said goodbye and told her he would be back.

The snow was falling ever so lightly, just like the inside of a snow globe, making it feel warm and cheery. Tony thought, better not let this interfere with my belief, no Christmas, no happiness, and forget celebrating birthdays. I'm just here for a quick visit, then it's off to somewhere warm where Tony could forget all about this nonsense. So Tony headed east on 5th Avenue until he hit Main Street. The first thought was this hasn't changed much in 30 years. Brought back some memories of when he was a young lad of 15 years. The five-and-dime stores were lit up like the 4th of July, looking south on Main Street. Colored lights everywhere, music blaring from every storefront. People rushed from shop to shop to find the perfect gift for loved ones. Shoppers were everywhere.

Tony headed south and jostled through the crowds while heading to 1st Avenue. He could make out the lake's shoreline, and the breeze from the lake was bitterly cold. He sucked up his collar to try and stay warm. In a couple of weeks, Tony would board the plane and head to Mexico, warmth and relaxation of the tallest order coming his way. Tony crossed at the traffic lights heading east. Once across the Street, Tony could go east or head north back into the throng of people, the endless noise, and the commercialization of Christmas. He stopped and looked east; the Street in front of him intrigued him. No hustle or bustle, no music, no lights, creating a fun atmosphere. Just a couple of shining stars in the east sky, down this darkened street that everyone had forgotten about.

Tony hesitated momentarily; which way to go, return to the hustle-bustle or find out what was down this dark street. But instead, he was intrigued and sucked up his collar to ward off the cold from the lake. Before Tony knew what was happening, he was heading east down this dark roadway, unsure why. Still, something was drawing him in this direction.

Tony continued to head towards the stars. After walking for five minutes, the Street seemed to get darker. This area was devoid of spirit. Finally, after ten minutes, he arrived where the stars had directed him, and some lights came into view. It was an old church steeple standing like a lone sentinel guarding the souls of the less fortunate. He recognized the area; the church of the Heavenly Saints had died, just as his parents did all those years ago. Tony noticed the sign on the front entrance, which said the church was closed, but the Lost Soul's Soup Kitchen in the basement was open.

Stairs went up to the main floor, where soul salvation occurred years ago. Another set of stairs went down into the depths of hell where a person might sell their soul for a hot meal. People were standing on the stairs waiting for the doors to open so they could go in and get a warm meal to nourish their bodies for one more night.

He was curious to see what was happening inside this place, and he decided to see if he could find another entrance. After all, he wasn't doing anything else; it was this, or he would return to the hotel room and wait for a new day. A side door with a sign says door locked; please use the front entrance. Tony figured he would try the door; it opened. Fortunately, the last person in had not shut the door tight; as a result, he snuck in. In front of his eyes was a kitchen with about fifteen people working various jobs. They were preparing to feed the lost souls standing outside, waiting to come in.

A woman busily moved from place to place. Talking to the people, she seemed to be in charge of getting this rag-time band of volunteers ready to feed the onslaught of lost souls coming for a meal.

She was black as ebony, heavyset, with curly black hair that went wherever it wanted. Yet, with a smile, this woman brought warmth to all the people she touched. As she barked orders to keep this rag-time band of souls moving in the right direction, people smiled and laughed as they moved in unison under her guidance.

She spotted Tony by the door, "Who are you, how did you get in, and what's your business here."

Tony was flabbergasted. Blurted, "I was just wondering if you needed any extra help, but I can see you have a full complement of helpers."

"Nonsense," she said, "go to the table with all the buns piled high. Start slicing and put a bun on a plate with a slab of butter. As the people walk by, hand them a dinner plate with a bun and offer encouragement if you have any. By the looks of you, I'm not sure what side of the table you should be on. Do you think you can handle that?"

Tony replied, "Yes."

Tony was on guard not to let anyone know that he was well off. Some of these people were souls that lost their way, while others were just down on their luck. The volunteers were just regular folk lending a helping hand during this time. Coming into Christmas, it was the year that everyone should be offering a helping hand. Thinking back to the orphanage, this was the time he despised, although he always enjoyed the special meal.

The woman in charge came over to see how he was doing, and Tony responded, "he was doing fine. What do they call you?"

She looked at Tony and said, "Her name was Annabel Heaven. Time to get to work. Harry, open the doors."

The crowd moved in. Lined up in an orderly fashion and got a hot meal, soup, and a bun with a hot cup of coffee and a warm spot to sit for a while. Then, in a couple of hours, the rush was over. The majority of the crowd disappeared into the night. Some had a spot at the shelters; some would be left on the Street.

In a couple of hours, everyone was served. Approximately one hundred people came in and had soup, a hot cup of coffee, and some conversation in a warm setting. The lost souls then disappeared into the night. People from every walk of life who were just down on their luck. Singles to families and everything in between brought back memories from the orphanage. In a split moment, his life was changed forever.

About an hour before the doors closed, a young woman with two young children quietly entered the establishment like they did not want to be noticed. Tony noticed her right away and wondered what her story was. Wondered why she was here, what happened. Of course, it was none of Tony's business, but an uneasy feeling overcame him. They came by Tony's station, received a bun and bowl, and then got a bowl of soup. Tony watched intensely. It made him sad to see this.

The evening ended, and Tony wondered what would be next. He grabbed a bowl and ladled some soup into it. Grabbed a bun and went and sat at the table so he could talk to Annabel. The soup was delicious, with chicken and vegetables and many spices warming the soul. Well, chatting with Annabel, Tony asked who made the soup?

Annabel smiled as she looked at Tony with piercing brown eyes that seemed to look right through him; "Well, the lord had his hand in it. Still, my African spice mixture is what brought it home."

Tony had another question for Annabel: Did she know anything about that young woman with the two children.

Annabel replied, "She had heard that the dad died a year ago from cancer. No other family to help her out;" Tony could relate to that. "The dad did not have insurance; they used all their savings to find a cure to no avail. Then the bank moved in and repossessed the house and belongings that had any value, then proceeded to throw them out on the Street."

Tony thought to himself, a sad story indeed.

Tony thought he had some free time before heading out on his next adventure to a warmer climate. So he asked Annabel if she could use help for the next few nights. Tony mentioned he had nothing but time on his hands for the next little while and was in between jobs. This was a little fib; Tony thought that was okay. He was guarding his identity.

Annabel replied, "Yes, if you are available, could you be here around one in the afternoon to help with the setup." As she spoke, "Annabel casually mentioned that help is always welcome, but she is unsure how long she can keep the soup kitchen open. Unfortunately, donations were running short, and the bank owned the church, which would be sold in the New Year. So, another location for the soup kitchen must be found; nothing was available in the area."

The night ended. Tony put on his parka, bundled up, bid Annabel good evening, and left the same way he came in. Annabel thought the Lord works in mysterious ways. This fellow seemed to be a strange duck; he listened intensely during their conversation. He looked like he should have been a patron of the soup kitchen, not someone offering to help. She couldn't put her finger on the odd feeling she was having. Oh well, I'm being guided by the Lord and not going to question the direction we are going in. Finally, Annabel shouted to her husband, Harry, "Time to go home, shut the lights off, and let's get going."

Tony made his way out into the night. As he was walking, he couldn't stop thinking about the woman with her two kids. A part of him was happy that he might see her tomorrow while, at the same time, hoping never to see her again. Hoping through all hope that something good would happen to her tonight and get her back on her feet.

Tony had heard in the conversations throughout the night. A new shelter on Fourth Street took in families, at least for a few nights.

Walking down the Street with snow crunching underfoot. Finally, Tony came to the corner. Saw a small sign with directions to the new family shelter's location and turned left three blocks down. For some reason, he made the turn and walked toward the building that offered hope for those needing a helping hand; he did not know why he made that turn, he did not know.

As Tony approached, he stayed in the shadows, not wanting to be seen. With the bright light on the door, he noticed the sign, New Light Family Shelter, all welcome.

Standing back in the shadows, he did not expect to see anyone at the door. Instead, the woman with the two kids stood at the door, ringing the buzzer to be let in. Finally, someone came to the door; she stepped in, the door closed, and they disappeared into the night. Watching them disappear into the building, Tony knew they would have a warm bed for the night.

Tony decided it was time to keep walking, making his way back to Main Street; very quiet now as most of the shoppers had gone home. The downtown area was still lit, looking down the Street, twinkling lights, music blaring, and the smell of money; this was the new Christmas. But Tony thought to himself a few blocks away, there was another Christmas taking hold. This one was darker and smelled of despair all around.

Tony returned to his room, lay on the bed, and thought about what had happened. He had an excellent evening, helping people who needed a lift and a warm meal. But, before long, sleep took over; there were no dreams, just a fitful sleep, wondering what would happen to the soup kitchen if no one was there to help.

In the morning, Tony woke with a start. He decided to support the soup kitchen, but he was unsure why. Just thought it was the right thing to do. Tony knew the soup kitchen could use food, so he dressed and went shopping.

Found the market he was looking for, Antonio's Italian Market, the same place it was so many years ago. He walked in the door. It had been years since he entered this little gem. He remembered going to the market at Christmas with his father and mother. They always had a great selection of food. The smells that wafted out of the back made him think of the fond memories he had with his parents, a part of his past he had forgotten but now would become part of his future.

A younger couple, the people running the store, Tony wondered if this was the son of the fellow who owned the store when his parents died. He introduced himself as Antonio Barbossa and discovered he was dealing with Giuseppe (Joe) and Angelina. Tony remembered Giuseppe. He was four years old the last time he had seen him.

Joe looked Tony over; "What is your name."

Tony replied, "Antonio Barbossa."

"Your name is very familiar," Joe commented. He had heard about the Barbossa family, who were killed in a car crash several years back on Christmas Eve. They had a younger son who became an orphan, had no family here, became a ward of the state, and moved away.

Tony looked at Joe and replied, "What a small world. I'm looking to place a food order for the soup kitchen on Fourth Street. Do you know the place?"

"Yes, I know it; we have donated to the Christmas dinner for the last few seasons."

Looking at Joe, Tony commented, "Could you deliver the goods to the soup kitchen by one p.m. today."

"Yes,"- commented Angelina. "Joe will do it himself."

Angelina looked at Tony, assuring him this would not be a problem.

"That's wonderful, and no one is to know who donated this food. The next thing I would like to do, if possible, is to open an account."

Joe looked at Tony and said, "My dad, God rest his soul; he used to have an account for everyone. But, unfortunately, times have changed, and we no longer do that."

Tony looked at Joe and said, "Can we compromise. You open an account for me, and I will pay an amount upfront."

Joe looked up and said, "You want an account, but the account will run with a credit to draw from."

"Yes."

"I think that can be worked out," Joe looked at Angelina for approval, and Angelina commented, "It's done."

Joe looked at Tony. The boss has spoken, "Whose name should I put on this account?"

Tony replied, "Antonio Barbossa and Annabel Heaven. I will let you know when we can activate Annabel's name. But, I want to keep this quiet and not a breath to anyone outside these walls."

Tony provided Joe with his list.

Joe looked it over and "said he could provide everything on it."

Tony bundled up, walked out the door, and told them on his way out, "he would be back in a while to square up the account."

Tony found the Thundering Waters Bank, walked in, and introduced himself to the manager (Harold Grabfy). This fellow fell all over himself and tried to make Tony comfortable. From the night before, Tony noticed the mom and the two kids from the soup kitchen. They were waiting to see someone in the waiting area. He asked the manager who she was, fully expecting that there would be no answer; this manager does not know what confidentially means. Before long, his mouth spewed words like diarrhea, trying to impress Tony on how much in the know he was.

The bank manager told Tony, "Joan, Johnny, and Lucy Rivera." The family had fallen on hard times, and her husband had passed away a year or so back, sick with cancer. So they did not really have much of a future."

The tragedy that struck the family put the bank's plan in play to recoup as many assets as possible. But, in the bank's wisdom, they decided the only option left was to foreclose on the property and put the Rivera's out on the Street.

Harry then looked at Tony and said, "Excuse me, but I have to deal with Rivera's; get them to come back at four p.m. this afternoon to sign the final documents. I will be right back."

Joan was unhappy with this ultimatum but knew she had no choice. So she asked, "What am I supposed to do."

Harry looked at her and said, "That's not my problem. I'm protecting the shareholders, our customers, and the bank's assets." Then, he turned, walked away from Joan, returned to where Tony stood and waited.

As he approached Tony, he politely said, "As you can see, we are here to take care of your money. We will not let anything happen to it. I must say we have come out of the Rivera relationship breaking even. So we consider it as a win for the bank."

Tony commented, "Not much of a win for the Rivera family."

Harold Grabfy continued to talk to Tony for some time about the Rivera family. He mentioned they would be back to sign the final documents this afternoon, giving the bank complete ownership. The family was hoping to get a little cash from this deal. Harold explained to Tony that they were in for a rude awakening: after interest and penalties, there was no cash. Tony thought about this for a minute; not really his problem; somehow, he felt he was doing enough helping out the soup kitchen. After all, he didn't come here to try and save the world; it was just a stopover for a few days. Tony felt helping the soup kitchen would be enough.

Tony politely stopped Harold from talking and stated he needed a thousand in cash and a certified cheque made out to Antonio's Italian Market for two thousand dollars. Harold, being the inquisitive type, asked Tony what this was for. Tony looked at him with steely eyes, and no word was spoken; Harold said he would get right on it, and it would not take more than five to ten minutes. Tony received the cheque, and the transaction was complete. However, there was one more thing he wanted to do. Tony went to a teller's window and told her he would like to deposit one thousand dollars into Joan Rivera's account. Within a few minutes, it was time to leave the bank. Tony bundled up again and left the establishment. He went out the door, leaving Harold still talking and reminding Tony that his bank would be more than willing to take care of his money. Tony thought to himself, this manager is a terrible man without empathy. It's time to get his finances in order and all accounts transferred to the Royal Blue Bank. This bank Tony had used before and will be the go-to establishment for the future. On his way to the market, Tony stopped at the Royal Blue Bank and made an appointment to see the manager at ten AM the next day.

As Tony entered the market, he saw Joe and Angelina working on the order. Preparations were well underway. The store felt warm and cozy; a calming feeling came over Tony. Not realizing just how much Harold Grabfy had set him off.

Joe looked at Tony and asked him, "Are you okay? You look quite a sight".

"Yes, fine," answered Tony. "How's the order coming."

"Coming great," replied Angelina.

"Okay, let's get this account set up." Tony looked at Joe and commented, "Here is a two thousand dollar certified cheque made out to you; how long do you think it will last."

Joe replied, "For sure, at least a week, maybe even longer."

"Great, I will be in and out, but if you need me for anything, you can reach the Thundering Waters Hotel, room 235."

Joe said, "Thank you for your business. If you need anything else, talk to us. I'm sure we will be able to help."

Tony thanked them for everything they had done but reminded them of the secrecy required to keep this venture moving forward.

They both replied, "Ciao as Tony stepped out the door."

Tony thought this ruse would continue until Annabel realized something mysterious was underfoot. Then she would question Joe, and he would spill the beans. Tony hoped he had a few days before this happened.

Tony went towards Main Street and decided to get to the soup kitchen at around two p.m. Did not want to be there when Joe dropped the goods off.

Walking down Main Street, the ambiance was a bit different. People were starting to shop. But it was not as chaotic as the previous night.

Tony did some window shopping and listened to the music coming from the speakers at the entrance of a couple of shops. A couple of hymns he remembered when he was young, Oh Holy Night and Silent Night. Thinking about his mother, he returned to reality as the song ended. What was happening to him? He was starting to care; he couldn't have that. He thought about Joan and her two kids. Even though he felt that her dilemma was not his problem, what would become of them.

Tony got to the corner, turned left, and walked down the street. Returning to where the blinding stars were in the sky the night before.

Tony arrived, went through the same door, and entered the kitchen. He saw Annabel and said hello. She looked him over and said, "You haven't found a barber yet. You still don't look like you should be on my side of the counter."

He proceeded to get ready and start with the job he had done the previous evening. Annabel stopped and asked if he could help Harry put the groceries away. She was flabbergasted. Where did all this food come from? This was not her regular order. That had arrived before this order and was already put out.

She knew the groceries came from Antonio's Italian Market. Still, there was no bill; the driver, Joe, who owned the market, delivered the goods and told Annabel he was ordered to do a delivery. Again, Annabel thought, no charge; mysterious things were happening. So, when she had a free moment, she would contact the market and get information about this order. She had enough food for at least a week or more. The Lord does indeed work in mysterious ways.

Tony walked over to where Harry was putting away the groceries. There was more food there than he had ordered. He will talk to Joe about that tomorrow. Annabel's little cooler was packed within a half-hour, and the dry goods area was overflowing with goods. Looking at what this goodwill effort had accomplished brought a smile to Tony's lips.

Annabel had the soup cooking. The aroma wafted out all over the kitchen and the dining area. Annabel commented that it smelled like heaven as far as she was concerned, and her patrons would be hungry once their senses got a whiff of what was cooking. It was now three o'clock, and Tony decided to go for a walk and return at six.

He noticed the new sign. Building for sale; contact Harold Grabfy at the Thundering Waters Bank. So Tony thought to himself, Harold Grabfy, true to his word, creating more hardship. The building belonged to the bank, and Harold wanted to unload it.

As Tony walked away from the church, he thought, this is not my problem. I have already done enough. I have given my time and bought food for the shelter. He was only in Thundering Waters to finish closing the finances on selling his property to Two Jacks Mining Corporation. Then, maybe have a quick look around the old place where he was born; after that, it would be time to leave.

Tony went to Main Street and Vi's Tavern for a meal. Walked in and cleaned the snow from his boots; just as he walked in, he heard a voice, "Just a minute, I'll be right there."
Tony looked around the place; there was another table with customers. A young couple sitting enjoying a meal, looking like they were in love, eating their spaghetti, reminding him of a Walt Disney movie Lady and the Tramp. He sat down in the same spot as the night before. Within a few minutes, she came out of the kitchen, a cigarette still dangling from her lips, looking like the same

T-shirt from yesterday. The apron was a little cleaner. She came over to where Tony was sitting.

"You again." Tony heard her comment, "What's a matter you, dona you know how to read? The sign says wait, I comin to seat you."

Tony apologized, "he would move. Where would she like him to sit?"

"Never you mind, you here now stay. Whata you want to eat. My specialty."

Tony interrupted, "No, I will have spaghetti and Italian sausage."

"Thata a gooda choice, but with sausage be one dollar more."

"That's fine."

"Okay, I will be a minute, to drink okay chianti it is."

Tony thought he would have preferred a beer, but he would just accept the wine instead of recurring the wrath of his host.

She brought out his meal, looked at him, and asked, "You got money; you look like someone who lives on the street."

Tony quietly finished his meal, asked for the bill, and placed the cash under his plate. Leaving a sizable tip, he quietly left with a smile.

Tony left Vi's Tavern and looked at his watch as he stepped out into the brisk evening air. Time to make his way back to the soup kitchen.

As he walked, Tony pondered the last few days. He sold his stake in the Blackwater Venture, came to Thundering Waters, and was drawn to a soup kitchen. Before he knew it, he was volunteering; he decided the kitchen needed some financial help, which he could provide. The last few days have been anything but boring. Tony wandered down Main Street. Woolworths, five and dime, was still here. Tony walked in to see if anything had changed over the years while he had been gone. The old hardwood floors creaked as he walked in and stamped his feet to knock snow off his boots.

The counters were jammed-packed with goods. Christmas music could be heard all over the store, cash registers ringing, clerks bustling and helping anyone who needed it. Old Spice shaving kits, socks, perfumes, candy, and other goods for this particular time of the year. The short-order counter on the right was full of shoppers ordering burgers, fries, and meatloaf with mashed potatoes and soda pop to wash it down. The smell permeated throughout the store. Tony wandered up and down the isles just looking and realized what Christmas had become: a commercial enterprise full of glitz and glamour. But, of course, the most important thing on the agenda would be gifts wrapped in colored paper and placed under the Christmas tree. Christmas morning presents are to be opened, Christmas dinner will be held, and maybe a visit to the church for Christmas service. Then there would be the people he had met the night before looking for a warm spot and a hot meal. Somehow, that thought was not sitting well, so he left the store.

Tony arrived at his turn and looked down the Street. The stars he could see were not as bright as the previous night but were still calling him.

You know what? Tony thought a commercial Christmas might not be so bad. Look at me; I haven't celebrated since I left the orphanage. I don't celebrate my birthday; I have too many bad memories. So let's go with the flow and help for a bit, then leave in a week and head to the warm climate, not knowing when he would be back.

Tony arrived at the kitchen, made his way to his station, and was ready to give a little warmth and encouragement to the patrons of this establishment.

Annabel made her way over to Tony's station, looked at Tony, and commented that the Lord does work in mysterious ways. But if you are an angel sent by the good Lord, you are the saddest-looking angel I have ever laid my eyes on. By the way, we will have to talk after we wind down tonight. I had a good chat with Guissepie from Antonios Italian Market. He had some remarkable things to say. For example, when I looked at the order this afternoon, there was so much food. I thought to myself when I talk to Guissepie, I'm sure he will let me know where it came from.

Tony looked at Annabel and decided the cat was out of the bag, so to speak. He knew that Joe would not be able to keep the secret. The lost souls were starting to form in a line at Tony station. Annabel looked at him and reminded him we would chat later. Tony nodded and proceeded to hand out buns, butter, and whatever else he had at his station.

The evening went smoothly when Tony saw Joan and her two kids enter. They took a seat in the corner so they would not be bothered by anyone and would not upset anyone. So they settled in, removed their jacket, and went to the area where they could get the buns and soup. Joan stopped and looked at Tony. "I saw you in the bank this morning; you talked to that awful man, Harold Grabfy."

Tony thought about denying it, but what good would it do. Tony sensed that Joan was the inquisitive type. He looked at Joan and waited for the next question.

Joan looked at Tony and commented, "You must be down on your luck. Harold Grabfy must've been giving you bad news, also." Finally, the question came, "What was he taking away from you. He took everything from us and left us a couple of dollars to try and survive on."

Tony looked at Joan, "He was not a very lovely person." Tony decided it was time to steer this conversation in a different direction.

"What is your name?"

"Joan Rivera, these are my kids, Johnny and Lucy."

Tony knew this information already, but the conversation was going differently, just as he had hoped. "When I'm on my break in a few minutes, I would love to chat with you."

Joan looked at him, puzzled. Alarm bells are going off in her head. But she blurted out "yes" before her brain got into gear.

Tony said, "Great," now he could chat with Joan, finish his shift, and skip out on Annabel. He could eliminate Annabel's questions, at least for the time being. Tony served a few more patrons, and his line was dissipating. Tony looked up and noticed there was no one at the station. Decided it was time to go and chat with Joan. He grabbed a coffee and moseyed over to where Joan was sitting.

"Hi there, mind if I sit down."

Tony thought on his way over to where Joan was seated. Who is this lady, really.

"Sure, grab a seat." Both kids said, "Hello,"

Tony acknowledged them and said, "Hello." This conversation is going to be cumbersome, Tony thought. But, being out of circulation with ordinary people, Tony was more in tune to have a business conversation than general chit-chat.

However, Joan knew he was having trouble and decided she would start the conversation. Joan looked at Tony and said, "How did you end up working here?"

Tony thought for a moment and told her about being in between jobs. He was out for a stroll and stopped on the corner, and he could see these two stars. It was like they drew him in. Something was calling him to check it out. So he proceeded to walk to the light. Once he arrived, Tony found the side door open and snuck in. Annabel saw him and asked what he wanted. Tony blurted out I'm between jobs and thought you might need help. Annabel said okay and told him he looked like he belonged on the other side of the table, but she would not turn him down. Tony told her he could be available for the next few days as he did not want to commit to a more extended period.

Tony looked at Joan and asked, "How did you end up in this predicament."

Joan replied, "It's a long story. The short version, I met my husband several years ago. They both were working at Black Falls Construction Company."

Tony knew the name; they worked on the mine site.

Joan continued on. "He was a construction superintendent, and she was in accounting. They crossed paths several times, and he finally asked her out. From there, they got married and had kids." Joan said, "She quit her job to give the kids a good start in life. Unfortunately, her husband got sick and was later diagnosed with stage four brain cancer. There was no cure. There was nothing that they could do about it. Exhausted their savings and quit making payments looking for treatment. None to be found. In a year, he peacefully passed away. We just got over the burial and other things associated with the death and received a letter from the bank. We had thirty days to make our payments to bring everything into order. That's when I realized we were in trouble with the bank. The bank and Harold Grabfy knew that was not going to happen. On the 30th day, we received an eviction notice. Whatever the bank had an interest in, they seized. They gave us two days to vacate, or the sheriff would be called in. That was a fine Christmas gift for us a week ago, and now you know my story."

Joan spent forty-five minutes telling the story. She needed someone to sound off on.

Tony asked her where you are going to stay tonight.

Joan replied, "Back at the shelter."

With that, Tony bid farewell and decided it was time to leave for the evening. Tony looked around for Annabel. She was nowhere to be seen; it was time to escape rather than face the inquisition from Annabel. Grabbed his jacket, slipped it on, and headed to the side door when he heard a mighty voice. "Where do you think you're going." Tony replied, "He had to leave and take care of some business."

Annabel replied, "I thought we were going to chat."

Tony said, "Maybe tomorrow if you still need some help."

Annabel replied, "Okay, see you at four p.m., and we will make time for that chat we missed today."

Tony said, "Okay," as he headed out the door into the cool evening air. It was snowing now. As he returned to the main street, with the snow gently falling, Tony felt like he was walking in a snow globe. Reaching his destination, he went to his room and crashed for the evening.

Up early the following day, Tony showered and went down for breakfast. While eating, thoughts of helping people in need kept nagging at him. Tony was well off now with a substantial bank account. He had plenty for himself, not enough to try and save the world. He had an angel on his shoulder whispering that no one was asking him to save the world, maybe just a tiny part. Not my problem, Tony thought, got up, left the restaurant, and returned to his room. He had to prepare for his appointment with the bank manager at the Royal Blue Bank. After meeting with the bank, Tony decided it would be time to chat with Joe and Angelina at the Italian market. He would find out how much Joe and Angelina spilled to Annabel. He smiled and wondered how much pressure Annabel had placed on him to get the information she wanted.

Tony grabbed his jacket, bundled up, and headed to the bank. The snow had stopped, cars were moving around, and Tony wondered where everyone was going. It was a brisk morning, so it should be. It was the middle of December, and winter had set in.

Tony entered the bank, walked up to the receptionist's desk, and told the receptionist he was there for his ten o'clock meeting with the bank manager. The receptionist looked at him. Tony could read her mind, yeah, right? So this guy has an appointment like I have purple hair.

"Please, just one minute, I will check with Mr. Luckseno to see if he is free. Your name, sir."

"Antonio Barbossa."

"Mr. Barbossa, Mr. Luckseno will see you now." She walked him to his office and announced, "Mr. Barbossa, to see you."

"Thank you, Rosemary, that will be all. Please close the door on your way out." Rosemary left and closed the door behind her.

"Sit down, Antonio. May I call you Antonio?"

"Yes, that's fine."

"Now, what can I do for you?"

"Well, Eric," Tony looked at the nameplate on his desk. "May I call you Eric?"

"Yes, by all means." Replied the bank manager.

Tony looked at Eric and started his story. "I am the sole owner of Eagle Mining and Prospecting Corporation. Recently, I sold one of my main assets for a large sum."

"Ah, yes," Eric replied. "I recently read about this sale in the Mining of the North magazine this morning. So you're the fellow."

"Yes."

"What kind of assets are we talking about."

"Mostly cash north of ten million."

"Eric whistled," We surely can help you out.

Eric looked at Tony and said, "All right, where do we start."

"Well, I have had a business account with your bank for some time. My assets are being held at the Thundering Waters Bank, and I wish to get these transferred to my business account. Would also like to open a personal bank account. I would like to deposit some money into this account. Over the next few days, I would like these assets transferred to my business account. Then close all business with the Bank of Thundering Waters as soon as possible."

Eric replied, "I will open the personal account right now."

"That's great. I will be back to transfer money into this account."

Eric looked at Tony, "Is there anything else I can do for you?"

While having breakfast this morning, Tony thought he should buy the church. Then, remodel the upstairs, turn it into offices, and leave the soup kitchen where it is. Although he thought about doing this, he wasn't sure why. He knew he could do it. It seemed to be the right thing to do.

"Yes, I need you to work on a project I have in mind. I have a numbered company that's already set up, and there is a purchase I would like to make." "Eric, are you aware of the soup kitchen on Fourth Street?"

"Yes, I am. That building just went up for sale. The Bank of Thundering Waters is the owner."

"I would like to purchase the church, but I need someone to buy the property. I don't want them to know who is making the offer. I want to ensure that Thundering Waters Bank does not profit from this sale; maybe breakeven would be okay. Do you think your bank can help me with purchasing this property? I would like to move very quickly. We would use my numbered account to facilitate the transaction."

"Yes, let me look into it. Give me till this afternoon to see what I can come up with."

Tony glanced at Eric as he left. "That will be great. I will be back around two this afternoon. One other thing, these dealings have to be kept very quiet."

22

Tony left the bank and walked over to the Italian Market. Stepping into the store, he saw Angelina at the counter.

Angelina saw him and said, "Hello."

Tony acknowledged the greeting and asked, "Is Joe at the back."

Angelina replied, "Yes, he is working on a meat platter."

Tony looked at Angelina, "Did you have a visitor yesterday."

"Yes," Angelina said in a quiet voice.

Tony tried to show some displeasure in his voice, not having much luck. Finally, as he strode to the back of the store, he called Joe's name. He could see Joe kinda hiding behind the counter. Joe looked like a kid caught with his hand in the cookie jar.

"Joe, come out; we have to have a talk." Tony heard a soft reply.

"Okay, I'ma coming." Joe fell into his broken English when he got nervous.

Tony looked at Joe, "Tell me, did you have a visitor yesterday."

"Yes," he replied, "it was that dark woman from the soup kitchen. She looked at me with those dark eyes like they were peering into my soul. As she spoke, she said, I have some questions for you. I looked at her and tried to match her stare, but I was no match. She had an evil hold on me. The first question she asked was, who paid for the grocery order. Although you did a good job camouflaging the order with what you donate weekly, I know it wasn't you. You must've thought I would just think it was your extra donation. But when I checked the order, I knew that many different items were added to your recurring gift. Although we have never formally met, Giuseppe, I know you. So, I'm going to introduce myself to you. My name is Annabel Heaven."

Tony patiently listened to what Joe told him, letting him proceed with his story without interruption.

"She told me she was from the darkest part of Africa. What she told me next, I knew I had to come clean."

The way Joe told the story, Tony knew he had listened intently to Annabel.

Tony looked at Joe. "Tell me what happened; what did she do that made you break our deal."

Well, Joe said. "She looked at me with large eyes and a smile. I have never seen teeth so white. Annabel noted, now you know who I am and where I'm from. So let's have a little chat. Guiseppe, it's said that I possess magical power from the darkest part of my homeland. I have never had to use them. But you might be the first to feel my wrath if I don't get the correct answers. She looked at me, and in a deep voice, she said, do you understand me. She scared me. I have heard about these people and wanted no part of her magic."

Tony had a hard time not laughing.

Tony realized that Joe was superstitious, so someone with Annabel's stature would easily scare the pants off Joe and possibly Angelina. Dark magic was heard about, especially in dark places around the world.

Joe looked at Tony and continued his story, and Tony was content to let Joe finish up. Joe said after Annabel looked at him and asked him the question, Joe felt he had no recourse but to try and tell Annabel something. Joe told Annabel that a stranger had come in and bought a bunch of groceries for the soup kitchen and asked Joe to have them delivered. He paid cash and asked Joe and Angelina not to say anything. Joe said while looking at Annabel; the gentleman was a stranger, that's all he knew, so he felt he would be no more help to Annabel. Joe said. Annabel looked at him and said Not so fast, Giuseppe; this gentleman bought all these goods paid cash, and you feel you cannot help more. That's right, Joe said. Annabel asked what the gentleman looked like. Joe knew he would have to say something. So, by telling a lie, the wrath of Annabel would be upon him.

Joe told Annabel the fellow that came in was about 6 foot tall with long brown hair and a scraggly beard. He looked like a homeless person. He almost asked him to leave the store when he first came in. Annabel looked at Giuseppe. Thank you for the information and the donation. I think I know who this person is. With that, Joe told Tony she looked at him and winked, then left the store. Tony looked at Joe, smiled, and said it was OK. Tony knew Annabel was formidable; he understood that she scared the pants off Joe. Tony looked at Angelina on his way out the door, smiled, and winked, letting her know everything would be okay. Joe looked at Angelina. I hope that's not the end of our relationship. Angelina looked at Joe and said no, it will be OK, he smiled at me on the way out.

Tony walked out; it was a beautiful sunny day. Heading to Thundering Waters Bank, he smiled. While thinking to himself, Annabel put the fear of God and the Devil into Joe simultaneously; there was no way he could not tell Annabel some information.

23

Tony walked into Thundering Waters Bank and got a hold of Harold Grabfy. Tony told Harold, "I need a cashier's check for one million dollars." Harold wanted to know why. Tony looked at him and told him, "It's my business, not yours."

Harold replied, "We are here to care for your money, so we don't want you to do anything stupid."

Tony replied, "Just get my draft ready." Thought to himself that it was a good thing his assets would be moved shortly. He really does not like this guy. A few minutes later, Tony was on his way out; as he left, he crossed paths with Joan. She was on her way in to finalize her dealings with the bank. They exchanged a hello as they both proceeded on their way.

Tony walked over to the Royal Blue Bank. Harold watched him from his window; now, what is he up to. Tony entered the bank. Eric Luckseno spotted him and came over right away. He said, "Hi."

Tony saw him and replied, "Hello, I have an envelope for you."

Eric took the envelope, walked to the teller, and asked her to deposit it into Mr. Barbossa's account. She did as instructed. "Let's go to my office and discuss the other project you have in mind."

They were seated in Eric's office. Eric told Tony for the church, the Thundering Waters Bank needs about eighty thousand dollars to break even. Tony thought briefly, "Okay, offer Thundering Waters sixty thousand for the church."

Eric looked at Tony, "When would you like me to make the offer."
Tony replied, "No time like the present. No conditions cash offer; the offer is good till tomorrow at 11:59 AM."

Eric picked up the phone and called Thundering Waters. "May I speak to Harold Grabfy, please?"

"Yes, just one moment. May I ask who's calling?"

"Eric Luckseno from the Royal Blue Bank."

Thank you. A few seconds later, Harold picked up the phone. "Hello, Eric. What can I do for you."

"You have a property listed, and I have a client interested in it, The Church of the Heavenly Saints." The one that has the Lost Souls Soup Kitchen in the basement. What is the bank trying to recoup on this property?"

Silence on the phone, Harold replied. Being greedy, he felt he had fish on the hook ready to be landed. "The bank must have at least one hundred and ten thousand dollars."

"OK," replied Eric; now listen carefully; I have a client willing to offer an all-cash deal with no conditions, sixty thousand dollars to purchase the church. The offer is good till tomorrow at 11:59 AM. Looking forward to hearing from you, remember Harold, don't be greedy. Goodbye."

Eric looked at Tony, "There, that's complete; now we will wait and see what he returns with. Anything else I can help you with today?"

"No," Tony stood, shook Eric's hand, put a jacket on, bundled up, and left the bank. Once outside, Tony wondered what he should do now.

24

Thinking, maybe just go for a walk to see the old house he remembered as a child. Wandering around the streets, Tony came across his old home; not much had changed. However, he could see a paint job was required, and probably some repairs were required, steps needed fixing, and the place was run down. But, remembering when he was young, it was a happy place; lots of memories were made there. Finally, it was time to walk back to the church. Tony figured he would stop at the five-and-dime store for a quick bite.

The sun was going down when Tony reached main street. The Christmas lights were coming on, and the music was as loud as ever. Tony entered a store that he had entered long ago. Nothing had changed. The dining counter was still on the right side. As Tony entered the store and looked around, a Christmas song came on: What Child is This. This song, one of Tony's favorites, was playing. It brought back memories from yesteryear and made him smile.

The five-and-dime store brought memories from long ago flooding his mind. Christmas was the farthest thing from Tony's mind a few days ago. Now, he seems to be right in the middle of it. The ambiance of the season is taking its toll on him. For years, this season never had meaning for him, a waste of time and a time that filled him with despair. Tony sat at the lunch counter, and an older woman came over and asked if he needed a menu.

Tony replied, "No, thank you. I will have a cheeseburger, fries, and a large cola."

"Coming right up," she replied.

Tony positioned himself at the counter so he could watch people do their shopping. People were hustling and bustling everywhere. It was the season to be jolly. Yes, he had not seen it for some time.

The cheeseburger arrived, a homemade patty piled high with cheese, pickles, lettuce, and tomatoes, just as he liked. The fries were crispy and hot, and the drink from the fountain machine was ice cold. Tony sat quietly and finished his lunch. He would have soup and a bun at the soup kitchen to tie him over to the following day. Tony finished his meal, paid, and left, heading to the kitchen.

G ot to the corner, looked down the street, and could see the two stars in the sky, but they were getting dimmer each night; Tony thought it must be an optical illusion. The funny thing was the lights were so bright on that first night, and now they seem to disappear into the night. Tony did not realize that his sad thoughts and rejection of the season caused the stars to fade. Tony had a dream. Somehow, he was responsible for saving the old church and soup kitchen. Purchasing the church made no sense. He was going to buy it, but why. Something was amiss, but Tony could not put his finger on it.

For years, Tony built up resentment and animosity toward this time of the year. He always wondered what kind of a God would take away his family. His life as he had known it. Subject him to a life without parents or family or lacking love and happiness. Yet, he never thought about his life's direction from that fateful night so many years before.

Tony arrived at the kitchen, walked in, spotted Annabel, went over to her, and asked her what she wanted him to do tonight. Annabel looked at Tony and thought, here is a soul who fits in with the lost souls she was serving. Whatever prompted them to meet up. She looked at Tony and said, I want you to work the floor tonight. Meet our souls and encourage them that things will get better.

Tony questioned this direction and told Annabel he would rather stay in the background.

Annabel looked at him and said, "No, this is what I need tonight, and before you leave, we will chat. If we don't talk tonight, then I think you have something to hide, and that's just not what I'm interested in."

Tony said, "OK," wondering why it was so crucial to Annabel for him to be to come out of his shell. So Tony grabbed a cart and decided he would do this. So he went on his way. Talking with some lost souls and offering encouragement. By the end of the evening, Tony was like a social butterfly chatting with everyone. Even stopped at Joan's table and chatted for a bit. This even brought a smile to Joan's face.

Annabel watched Tony throughout the evening. She thought there was more to this character than meets the eye. The Lord does work in mysterious ways. Annabel was happy that the good Lord had a plan. She knew that the church was up for sale. When sold, it could be the end of the soup kitchen. She was already notified by the Bank of Thundering Waters that they would have to vacate the premises by December 31. The soup kitchen would continue on, but where.

This location is excellent, only a few blocks from the shelter. Annabel felt God had a plan. Whatever happens, the soup kitchen will survive. Annabel thought she would take one day at a time. But, whatever happens, it will not be the end. Most of the souls who visited tonight had their meal, and the soup kitchen was clearing out.

She located Tony and said, " OK, let's sit here and chat. Tony agreed, got a coffee, and sat down with Annabel.

She looked at Tony and said, "You're not hungry tonight."

"No, I had a bite to eat before I got here."

Annabel looked at Tony with those huge brown eyes. Tony felt uncomfortable now he knew how Joe felt.

"You still look like a person who should be receiving instead of giving;" Annabel watched Tony's face, looking for any noticeable change. Tony offered no reaction to what Annabel had just said.

Annabel decided to go with a new direct approach. Trying to get Tony to open up. She looked at Tony and carefully said, "OK, who are you. I talked to Giuseppe, and he gave me a description of you, a man who purchased the food for the kitchen. I suspect that you are that person. I'm asking again: 'Who are you?"

Tony looked at Annabel and thought, how am I going to answer the question and make it believable. "I'm a prospector and have worked living in camps for the last couple of years. So, with no time off, I decided to come out and meet the rest of the world."

Annabel thought that could be why he was reluctant to get out on the floor and mingle with people.

"The first night in town, I was walking and found this soup kitchen accidentally. So I came in, and you spotted me. I asked if you needed any help. So you put me to work as you were running short of volunteers. As we talked during the night, you mentioned that the kitchen was running out of food, and I thought I could help. So I went to that

Italian Market and purchased food for the kitchen, my way of giving back."

Annabel looked at Tony, "OK, this is possible, but who are you? What made you come to Thundering Waters."

Tony looked at Annabel, "I got to the bus station with nowhere to go, so I decided Thundering Waters would be as good as any to visit. This was my hometown many years ago. We used to live here, but on Christmas Eve, my parents were killed in a terrible accident on the corner just outside your doors. So, I ended up as an orphan. I felt it was time to return and look at my hometown."

"While walking that first night, I saw two stars above the church from a few blocks away. Strangely, these stars had been following me for a few days. Nevertheless, it drew me to the church, and ultimately, I found the soup kitchen, so by making my way to the stars, I saw you, and the rest is history."

Annabel thought to herself, what lights could he be talking about. The church had no light that could be seen from a distance. There were no lights in the steeple either.

Tony looked at Annabel. "Any other questions. Oh, so you won't be surprised. There will be another order of food coming tomorrow."

Annabel looked at Tony, and all she could say was thank you very much.

Tony got up and helped others with the cleanup. Thought to himself, was that enough information for now. Annabel watched Tony like a hawk. What was his end game?

With the cleanup complete, Tony quietly slipped away, put his jacket on, and headed out. But, before going out into the brisk evening air, Tony went up the remaining stairs to see if the doorway to the main floor was open. He placed his hand on the door handle and turned quietly. The latch let go, Tony shoved gently, and the door opened. Stepping inside, Tony felt like he had walked into a time capsule; the main floor looked just as he had remembered it from so many years before. But now, the church was abandoned. Instead, Tony had heard a new one was built for the parishioners, fancier and full of glitz.

Tony stepped in; a few lights were on, and he could see the general layout. There were no changes; it looked the same. On his left was the pew he and his parents would like to sit at during the services. Tony again looked around the pews, stained glass windows, basically a blank canvas. Standing there, Tony felt he should fall on his knees and give thanks that he was still on this earth, having the opportunity to look at this building. Tony thought he was being watched, but not a soul was around. What was happening, and where did these thoughts come from. Tony was drawn back here. Strange things are happening.

Tony thought about this place. If I could get it for the right price. The church could be remodeled into an office complex and used as the new headquarters for Tony's company, Eagle Mining and Prospecting Corporation. He could keep the downstairs set up and continue with the Lost Soul's Soup Kitchen. That would be a load off Annabel's mind.

Again, Tony felt he was being watched. It was a feeling he couldn't shake, and slowly he turned around. To his surprise, Annabel stared at him. The dark brown eyes seem to be burning a hole through his soul. Again, Tony stared at Annabel, and finally, she spoke, "What are you doing up here."

"Nothing," came the response from Tony.

Annabel continued the conversation, "Just what are you up to? You look like a homeless person. But you act like someone not homeless but a soul with an agenda. So we will have to finish our conversation that we started downstairs."

"Annabel, you know my name is Antonio Barbossa. As I have told you, this was my hometown. I left here in 1955; I was sent to an orphanage after my parents were killed on my birthday, Christmas Eve. I finally returned to look at the old homestead and somehow found my way to you; I don't know why. Just give me till Monday, and we will sit and talk. I will fill you in on as much as I know. I'm not up to no good, I promise you that."

Annabel thought for a minute and then replied, "All right, I know something is amiss around here, and the good lord is not letting me in on his workings."

27

Tony left the church and headed back to his hotel room. Stopping on the corner and looking back, no light shone; Tony thought Annabel was right. Something is amiss around here.

Tony stopped at the Italian grocery and walked in. Joe was behind the counter.

"Good evening, Joe; how are you doing."

'Fine my friend, and you."

"OK," just a quick question: "Is the order already for tomorrow."

"Yes, it is," Joe replied, "it will be delivered at one p.m.."

"Good, take care, my friend," Tony stepped out into the brisk evening air and returned to the hotel.

There was a message at the counter for him. Eric from the Royal Blue Bank wondered if he could drop by the bank at 10 a.m.

Tony headed to his room. Once there, he decided a hot shower was what he needed. The hot water melted away the stiffness in his body and warmed his heart. Tony crashed for the evening, and just before sleep took over, he wondered what Eric wanted. Maybe Harold Grabfy came back with an offer.

28

In the morning, Tony headed for breakfast; taking his notebook, it was time to make a plan.

Tony thought today was an excellent day to formulate a plan to try and save this small portion of the world. He was not sure why. A thought kept telling him this was what he was meant to do. No matter what, he was flying south on the 23rd of the month.

Tony started his plan:

Meet with Eric Luskseno
See if Harold Grabfy has presented an offer. If he has, do we counter or purchase? To be completed by today, if possible.

If the sale is complete, find someone to renovate this afternoon. The plan is to remodel the main floor and set up offices for Tony's company. The project must include the steeple and keep as much of the older décor as possible, including the stained glass windows.

Downstairs, keep the Lost Souls Soup Kitchen functioning and do some significant renovations in the future.

Talk to Annabel tonight about the plan and tell her I can't help in the kitchen for the next three nights. Will have to fill her in on the long-term plans for the building. The upper floor will contain Eagle Mining and Prospecting Company offices and a spot for the Lost Souls Soup Kitchen Charity. Tony was hoping that Annabel would be able to run the charity.

Tony knew he needed help for his company as well. A great mining engineer would also be a bonus and someone to look after the financial side. It's too bad he didn't know where Adam was; he could be the perfect fit for this role.

This weekend, Tony decided to head east to visit a property he had acquired a few years back. They were setting up the place to do some work before spring came.

Tony felt giddy putting his plan together. He could remember what his father said: Always give back, Antonio, no matter how much you have, because someone is less fortunate than you. Tony felt somehow he had received a new lease on life, or would it be a curse? He wasn't sure but decided to ride the good feeling for a while. His plane ticket was bought. The plan had a beginning, an ending, and much work in between. It was time to enjoy life and continue on the journey he laid out.

29

Tony decided it was time to go and see Eric at the Royal Blue Bank. When he arrived, he was shown to Eric's office immediately.

"Good morning, Eric."

"Good morning, Tony. Well, I got a call from Harold from Thundering Waters Bank. He came back with a counteroffer. Harold said they would let the church go for Ninety Thousand Dollars."

Tony thought for a minute, then replied, "That's ridiculous. If they don't take our offer, this building will sit for the winter. So what I propose is we counter. Offer Seventy-Five Thousand dollars. Make the deal contingent on closing today by 12:59 PM. Again, no conditions."

Eric had anticipated Tony's reaction. He had the offer ready to go. All Eric had to do was fill in the numbers, the purchase price, and the time the offer closed. So he picked up the phone, called the receptionist, and asked her to run this offer over to Harold Grabfy at the Thundering Waters Bank. The task was to be carried out immediately as it was time-sensitive. She took the envelope and headed out. In a few minutes, Tony and Eric could see her entering the bank across the street. The offer was now in play.

"Tony, what are your plans if you get the building."

"Well, "I had a good look at the church. It seems to be a good building with lots of history, good and bad. So, I thought I would convert the upstairs to offices, making Thundering Waters my home base. Would also add one or two offices for the Lost Souls Soup Kitchen Charity."

Let me ask you a question? "Do you know any people who do renovations?"

"I know of one company called Creative Restorations, and they do fantastic work, I'm told. In fact, their shop is only a couple blocks south of the church."

"OK, thanks, Eric. I will check with you at 1 o'clock to see if there's an answer or any movement on our property proposition to Thundering Waters."

30

Tony left the bank and decided to find Creative Restoration. So, walking down the main street, he turned towards the church, then headed south until he arrived at a small shop with a sign above the door. Creative Restorations.

Tony opened the main door and stepped inside. Immediately, he could see and smell fresh wood and paint. It seemed like a busy place.

Tony approached the receptionist and asked if he could speak to the owner. The receptionist looked at Tony. Thinking now, what does this fellow want. Then she looked at Tony and said you're in luck. I've got a few minutes to talk right now. "What can I do for you?"

Tony, flabbergasted, looked at her and said, "I'm looking at purchasing some property, and it will need major renovations. It's a blank slate, and I want to take the main floor, remodel it into offices, etc. I'm thinking of relocating my company here."

The girl looked at him, puzzled. This fellow, she thought, doesn't look like he could have two nickels to rub together. Let alone purchase property and then go for major renovations. But, she thought to herself, looks can be deceiving.

She thought for a minute and decided to entertain his thought process for a while. She has nothing on the books right now, nothing ventured, nothing gained.

"OK," she said, "where is the property you are looking at."

"First things first, this has to stay between us. It can't be leaked at all."

Red flags rose, but she decided she would continue entertaining this fellow. "Yes, these conversations will stay between the two of us,"

"Okay, you know, the old church north of here, you can see the steeple out your back door."

"Yes, I know it well. It used to be my church years ago, but the people moved away, and ultimately the church closed down. I understand it is a soup kitchen for lost souls now."

"You are right. Do you think you could work some magic on this old structure?"

"Of course," she replied, "all it takes is money."

Tony looked at her and then proceeded into his vision. "The main floor, I would like to turn into offices, and in the middle, a boardroom, washrooms, and a small kitchen facility in the north corner. Would like to keep all windows if possible. I would like to use the windows that have to be closed due to construction constraints for doorways or partitions where possible. Then, plumbing and wiring must be brought up to code. The soup kitchen will require a significant update. This will occur in stage two, but the wiring and plumbing must be fixed now. We don't want to lose the importance of the steeple and will leave it to your creative thinking on how it will be utilized. So that's my rough vision. Does it scare you off?"

"No, not at all. I remember what both areas look like, and I will do some rough drawings over the weekend to see what might be feasible."

"OK, it's almost 1 o'clock, and I have an appointment at the bank to get to. I understand that you can't be doing this work for nothing. So, will a $1000 retainer be enough to get you started?"

She looked at Tony, "That will be fine."

Tony looked at her and counted out the cash.

She looked at him with a strange look. Who is this guy? From appearances, he seems like a bum, but on closer glance, his hair was washed, he has clean clothes, and he has a pocket full of cash. Tony said, "I will pop in for further discussion in a few days. Will that be ok?"

"Yes, that will be fine."

Tony got up and started heading to the door.

"By the way, my name is Mitch Brown."

With a smile, Tony replied, "How do you do, Mitch? My name is Tony Barbossa; see you later."

31

As Tony entered the bank, he could see Eric waiting for him.

"Well, Thundering Waters is interested in the proposal they returned with a counter." Eric offered the information.

Tony looked at Eric; "What did he have to say."

"Thundering Waters would like to counter with Eighty Thousand dollars."

Tony thought. This was a good deal. He looked at Eric and said, "Okay, let's get this guy on the phone and remind him our offer was final. Is he willing to let the building sit empty for winter for Five Thousand dollars? Tell him you have a cheque that can be delivered within 30 minutes."

Eric looked at Tony, "We have nothing to lose."

Eric picked up the phone and dialed Thundering Waters.

"Hello, how may I direct your call," replied the receptionist.

"Good afternoon. May I speak to Harold Grabfy, please," said Eric."

"Just one moment, may I ask who's calling."

"It's Eric Luckseno from the Royal Blue Bank."

"Just one minute, please, Mr. Luckseno. I will put you through now."

"Good afternoon, Eric. This is Harold speaking. How are you today."

"Just fine, Harold. The reason I'm calling is about the offer on the church. My client has instructed me to relay this message to you. Our existing offer of Seventy-Five Thousand dollars is firm and final. Would you let the building sit empty for winter for Five Thousand dollars? We can have a cheque for the total amount delivered within Thirty minutes."

"Eric, can I call you back in five minutes."

"Yes, that will be fine, any longer, and we will have to take our business elsewhere."

Within five minutes, Eric's phone rang. "Hello, Eric Luckseno speaking."

"Eric," Harold Grabfy speaking. "I have good news: We will accept your offer."

"Very good," replied Eric. As he was speaking, he glanced over to and looked at Tony with a smile and wink, and Tony knew that the deal was accepted. Eric is one step ahead of Tony. The documents were ready, with a cheque made to Thundering Waters Bank. The documents were signed.

Eric called the receptionist in. "Could you run this over to Harold Grabfy at the Thundering Waters Bank across the street? Please wait for the documents that will be forthcoming." The documents were gathered together, and the receptionist was on her way.

In the meantime, Eric told Harold, "Harold, you can expect the money shortly. Could you have the deeds ready to go?"

Within an hour, the receptionist was back with the documentation. Tony sat back and thought well, that's done. I bought an old church, so what's next. Tony hoped the For Sale sign would disappear as fast as he made his purchase. Decided he would have a chat with Annabel this evening. Just fill her in if need be. Then, in the morning, he will drive east for the weekend to visit a claim group he owned. He had crews preparing the property and getting ready for future exploration. It was a great afternoon. Tony said goodbye to Eric and headed back to his hotel room.

32

Tony thought he would get the hotel to fix him up with a rental vehicle for the weekend. Then, he went to his room and got his gear ready for his trip in the a.m. It was about a two-hour drive along the shore of the big lake. Tony looked around. He was prepared to go and decided it was time to go and visit Annabel. See what help she would need for the evening. So Tony headed out and made his way to the corner. This corner so far has had a profound effect on his life. Looking down the street, the stars to the east above the old steeple shone bright; Tony thought, why can no one else see these stars.

Why was he the only one drawn to these dam lights or stars, whatever they were? Maybe it was his parents' way of telling him to ensure he does something good with his newfound wealth. Tony ventured off, once again, towards the lights. It started to snow. As he walked, an eerie feeling came over him. What was he doing? The lights in the dusk looked like stars off in the distance. They were having a profound effect on his thoughts. He was starting to second-guess himself. He remembered how much he disliked this time of the year. Looking up, Tony saw the lights had dimmed. No longer were they shining with a promise that magical things and feelings would happen. When he arrived, Tony looked at the front of the church for the for sale sign. It was gone.

Thinking at least that part of the plan had worked, he bought an old church. Went to the side door and stepped in. Tony stopped and observed what was happening.

Annabel was busy getting the volunteers to their stations, bellowing out instructions gently. The volunteers scoured around like ants, all moving in different directions. At this time, Annabel looked over her shoulder and saw Tony standing, watching the proceedings.

"Tony, I will let you be the rover again."

"That's fine, Annabel. As I walked in, I noticed the for sale sign was gone. Did the building get sold, or did the bank decide now was not the time to sell?"

Annabel looked at Tony, "It got sold. I got a call from the bank this afternoon, and they told me it was sold. So, I have a number to call to see if they still want us to vacate the premises by December 31. It won't be hard to do; we just have to ensure that the food is mostly gone so that we have less to move when it's over. But, unfortunately, it was late in the day when I got the call from Thundering Waters Bank and too late to call the other number to find out the situation on vacating the premises."

The phone rang, and Annabel's husband, Harry, answered. "Annabel, it's for you."

Annabel looked at Harry, "Just take the number, and I will call back tomorrow."

"You better come and talk to this gentleman. He says it's essential that he speaks to you."

Annabel walked over to the phone, "Hello, Annabel Heaven speaking, how can I help you."

"Hello, Ms. Heaven. My name is Eric Luckseno from the Royal Blue Bank. I will get right down to business. I have a client who purchased the building you're currently occupying. I understand you are operating the Lost Souls Kitchen from this location. Am I right in this assumption?"

Annabel felt her heart race as she replied, "Yes, I am."

"Great," came the reply from the other end of the phone,

Annabel's mind was racing. She knew this was when he was going to ask that they vacate the premises as quickly as possible and no later than December 31.

Eric was speaking to Annabel, but she was not listening. Instead, she was trying to formulate a plan for her next steps.

Finally, Eric asked Ms. Heaven, "What is the agreement on vacating the building you have with the Thundering Waters Bank?"

"Please call me Annabel; we were told we must vacate the property by December 31."

"OK, are you paying rent?"

Annabel thought, "Yes, they charged us Five Hundred dollars monthly."

Eric listened intensely and noticed the sadness in her voice. Then, he replied, "I have some good news for you; my client has decided you can stay until the end of the first quarter of 1986, and no rent will be charged. But you'd have to be out by March 31. He thought that would give you more time to find a place. So, instead of shutting down in the middle of winter, looking for a new home in the spring might be less challenging. So, can you come to the bank to sign a new agreement?"

Annabel was flabbergasted, "Yes, I will be there."

Tony watched Annabel while she was on the call. He could see her face brimming with happiness. Tony knew what was happening as he had set this up with Eric.

Annabel hung the phone up and called Harry over. She was beaming like a ray of sunshine.

Annabel told Harry the news and hugged him, and Tony could see the smiles on their faces.

Annabel let go of Harry and returned to where Tony was waiting. When Annabel said just a minute, Tony was ready to start roving, talking, and greeting the lost souls. But first, I would like to tell you about my call.

Annabel blurted out, "Well, that was the best call I've gotten in a long time. It was a fellow representing the person who bought this building, and he passed on some information. The best is that we don't have to be out until the end of March next year. I have to go in and sign the documents sometime next week." She looked at Tony, "Isn't that fantastic news."

Tony looked at her, "I guess so, but you're just putting off the inevitable. You still have to move."

Annabel looked at Tony, "You know you're a guy with a glass that's half empty instead of half full."

Tony pretended he didn't know what she was talking about and looked at Annabel, staring into never neverland.

Annabel looked at Tony and commented, "This is terrific news. I knew the good Lord would not let me down at this time of the year."

Tony thought to himself as he started roving throughout the room. It's the good Lord, haha. She doesn't realize that Christmas came early for her because of a prospector who had lots of good luck. He decided to pass some good fortune forward. It had nothing to do with the good Lord and Christmas, two things Tony despised.

33

He was wandering among the tables when Joan and her two kids came in. Tony watched them get seated and walked over to see how they were doing. "Looks like we have had a little bit of good fortune. Tomorrow, we take possession of a little furnished apartment through the government grant program. So, at least we will have a roof over our heads at Christmas. We are getting some money to survive on at the end of the month. It's going to work out. I will be able to get the kids into a new school in the new year and be able to start looking for a job."

"That's great," commented Tony.

Also, we got a call from Harold Grabfy. He told us that our repossession was closed. There would be a little bit of money left for us.

Another work of art orchestrated by Eric Luckseno, Joan will have an extra thousand dollars to help out over Christmas.

Tony watched her. The kids got up and got a bowl of soup, a bun, and a glass of milk. He looked at Joan and said, "Good things come to good people." Tony still can't figure out what's going on with him. One minute, he's helping where he can, and then he's second-guessing his choices.

Tony looked at Joan and commented, "How would you like to go out for a meal on Monday night? I would say this weekend. Unfortunately, I must be out of town tomorrow and part of Sunday."

Joan looked at Tony, "I don't think so. I have the kids with nowhere to leave them."

"That's OK, bring them with you."

Joan looked at Tony, "Okay, I think we can make it."

"Do you know where Vi's Tavern is?"

"Yes."

"Good, I will meet you there at 4 PM on Monday evening."

"Thank you," Joan replied, "I will see you then."

34

Tony decided to catch Annabel and let her know he couldn't work for the next three nights and wanted to discuss the plans for Christmas Eve and Christmas Day dinners.

Annabel was sitting with Harry. They were discussing the phone call with Eric Luckseno.

Tony strolled over and asked, "Can I sit down for a moment."

Annabel replied, "By all means."

Tony sat and looked Annabel straight in the eye. He said, "I'm afraid the next three nights, I'm not going to be able to help you as I have to head out of town for the weekend. I'm visiting a mining camp east of Thundering Waters."

Annabel looked at Tony, "That was fine. She appreciated all the help and the donations of food, which made her life a lot easier."

Tony looked at Annabel, "There will be another order arriving tomorrow. I have arranged to have two more deliveries arriving over the next few weeks. If you run short, talk to Giuseppe at the Italian market and tell him what you need; he will take care of you.

Don't worry about the cost. It's just my way of offering a little help. My parents always said to help out the not-so-fortunate if I could.

Annabel thought for a moment. Tony mentioned his parents again. She felt he offered her a chance to ask more pointed questions about Tony and his life. She looked at Tony and decided now was the time to ask about Tony's life.

Annabel said, "Thank you from the bottom of my heart. This donation will go a long way. Where are your parents."

Tony looked at her, "As I told you, both have passed."

She was about to ask another question as she felt Tony might open up, but Tony changed the subject before she could.

Looking at Annabel, he calmly stated that Christmas was coming up. "Is the kitchen open on Christmas Eve and Christmas Day?"

Annabel stated, "We are usually open on Christmas Eve but never on Christmas Day. Harry and I could be here, but the lack of volunteers for Christmas Day creates a problem."

"Oh, I see, so what kind of meal do you cook on Christmas Eve?"

"Well, it depends on donations. We try to have a regular Christmas Eve supper for Lost Souls."

Tony looked at Annabel. "If you had the volunteers for Christmas day, I assume it would be much the same meal being served on Christmas Eve."

"Yes," Annabel answered in a quiet voice.

It would be fantastic to host both days, seeing how this is likely the last year of hosting here. I'm sorry I won't be able to help during this time frame as I will be gone from December 23rd till January 3rd. I will see what I can do. I might be able to get some people that I know to work both days.

Annabel looked at Tony, "We have plans, do we."

Tony casually looked up from his coffee and replied yes, snow is not even in the picture.

With that, Tony decided it was time to return to the hotel and get a good night's sleep. Tony looked at Annabel, said good evening, slipped his jacket on, and told Annabel he would see her in three days. When you meet with Guiseppe about your order, try not to scare him with your black magic. Annabel looked at Tony and winked, then let out a thundering laugh from her soul's inner depth. Tony closed the door behind him and headed to the corner where all this nonsense started. Once at the corner, Tony looked over his shoulder, and the stars shone with an intense glow. Why, he did not know, a message, he wasn't sure.

Tony turned the corner, returned to his hotel room, cleaned up, crawled into bed, and slept.

35

Got up the next morning, had breakfast and headed out. What a gorgeous day for a drive. The sun was shining, and the landscape was as white as possible. Whites and greens against a blue sky, a winter wonderland with magic that filled the air. Occasionally, he saw one of the many bays on the big lake. Ice was starting to form, and then there was the water, a deep wintery blue hue as far as the eye could see. Water marked the contrast between frozen land and a lake that has not slept yet. As he was heading east, he could see the sun coming up and the two stars that seemed to be guiding his way.

In a couple hours, Tony turned left onto an old logging road. He had another 15 miles to go and would be at the camp where his newest venture was starting to take hold. Tony arrived, parked, and then went into the office. A small trailer was set up to accommodate the business at hand. It was big enough for a couple of offices and a large room where maps could be set out to go over the work that would be forthcoming as time progressed. Tony opened the door and yelled, "Alfonso, are you here?"

"Yes, come in. Ah, Antonio, it's you. I wasn't expecting you for a couple hours yet. Let's store your gear and go to the lunch trailer, where we can have a cup of coffee and catch up. I have a new guy working here, a big fellow with a big, bushy red beard. This fellow says he knows you. Met you a few years back at the Dark Waters Venture site. Said he worked with you starting that property; I felt safe bringing him on. I couldn't figure out how he worked with you with a bum leg tramping all over the bush. Then he told me his story. He was in good shape when working with you. Then, a couple of years ago, he had a horrible accident and lost the lower part of one leg, so his days of tramping ended. Told me this all happened while working in the north, chasing gold. He came in looking for a job. The only thing I had at the time was a kitchen helper position. He told me that would be fine; he needed to work."

Tony could not believe what Alfonso was saying to him. Could this be Adam? He would know in a few minutes.

They walked into the dining trailer, the cooking area to the left with a serving counter and tables scattered throughout enough room for about forty men. It's a bit overkill right now, only ten in camp, but it could climb to twenty or more in the new year. In the corner was a nicely decorated Christmas tree. Tony guessed it was there to bring some Christmas spirit to the camp. Unfortunately, having Christmas spirit was not high on Tony's agenda.

Tony looked at the fellow behind the serving counter. He was facing the cooking area with his back to Tony. Tony could tell it was indeed Adam. "Well, young feller, what are you up to," Tony asked.

Adam heard the voice and recognized who it was instantly, commenting, "Six foot five and a half, look what the cat dragged in. How the heck are you, Antonio? You look good but still look like a person who doesn't have two nickels to rub together. Looking for work, are you? Too bad I got the last job here."

Tony looked Adam up and down. Tony had heard that Adam had a severe leg injury. Still, with no movement on Adam's part, Tony could not see what type of injury Adam had succumbed to.

Adam stood behind the counter, looking at Tony, not moving, not wanting to show Tony what he had done to himself.

Tony and Alfonso grabbed a coffee and went and sat down at a table. Tony looked at Alfonso, "How is fieldwork coming along?"

Alfonso explained, "Slow right now. The daylight was short, but we had a couple of good months previously. The line cutting and setup for geophysics for the subsequent fifty claims should be complete by mid-January. But for sure, by the end of January. The geophysics crew will arrive in mid-February, and their part will be completed in one month. The drilling crew will come at the end of February. They will set up at the discovery outcrop and drill their first hole. This work should carry through until Spring arrives. Once spring is here, we will take at least a couple of weeks off. When we return, the geophysics targets will be located, and we will drill earnestly. This will take us till summer's end. By then, we will know if there will be a new discovery and possibly a new mine." Tony listened intently, noting that Adam had snuck out for a break and returned to his room for a few hours, waiting for the crews to come in from the field.

Tony asked Alfonso, "When are you shutting down for Christmas."

"Our last day of work will be December 20. The majority of the crew will leave on December 21.

Part of the crew has nowhere to go as they move from camp job to camp job. I will hold back these fellows for one day to help with the camp shutdown, and then they will leave on December 22. Our operations base will be shut down until January 5. Then, we will open the camp, and crews will return on January 6." Alfonso looked at Tony, "Can you see any problems?"

Tony thought, then asked Alfonso, "Do you expect them to return after the Christmas break? Are they a good crew, and would you like to keep them together?" Tony knew continuity was essential to make the job a success."

"Yes, they are a good crew, no troublemakers. But I'm afraid if I cut them loose. I will lose at least half. I'm sure the ones going home to their families will be back. The others, I'm not sure about."

"OK, let's pick this problem up later. Let's head back to the office. You can show me the plan. Tony had staked the area a few years back, did the initial prospecting, and had an idea of where he wanted to start the geophysics program. So Tony and Alfonso retreated to the office. Alphonso spread the plan on the table, and the two men locked eyes on the project's direction.

Around 4 p.m., it was dark, and Tony walked to his room to get cleaned up for the evening dinner. He stopped and looked up at the sky. He felt he could reach out and touch the stars. His stars in the east were shining bright, as was the north star. A star Tony had used to find his way back home on many an occasion. Now, it seemed he had another group of stars toiling to take him in a foreign direction. Tony shook off the uneasy feeling and entered his room.

38

Alfonso banged on his door, "Tony, are you ready."

"Yes," came the reply, "just give me a minute." Tony acknowledged Alfonso, and they headed to the dining trailer together. Tony admired the stars again. The sky seemed to be full of diamonds. The only sound that could be heard was the generator providing power to the camp. Tony stopped and thought momentarily and told Alpfonso how far we have come from the good old days. Kerosene lanterns, tents, and wood stoves for heat. Tony had moved from tents to hotel rooms and camp trailers in a few years.

They entered, and no one gave Tony a second thought. The crew did not know Tony was the owner. He had some lesser claims in the area that he had picked up in a land swap with another project. Tony spun these claims off for cash, using this money to fund this venture.

They grabbed a table in the corner; hopefully, they would not be disturbed. Tony and Alfonso moved to the serving line to get their evening meal. Receiving his meal, Adam dished up his spuds and vegetables. Tony looked at Adam and said, "What time are you finished."

Adam commented, "Not till late."

"We have to have a chat."

Adam looked at Tony, "Nothing to chat about."

Tony noticed Adam not moving very much. So, he got himself into a position where he could serve the people without placing any stress on his leg. Tony was standing there. The lineup was getting long, so Tony got the remaining portions of his meal and moved on.

Tony went and sat with Alfonso. "This meal looks fantastic."

"I hope it is," replied Alfonso, "an old manager I met once told me if you want happy people in a camp, feed them well."

Tony chuckled. He remembered one of his early camp jobs; they had an old bushwhacker for a cook. Little did anyone know this guy only had one specialty. Everything was cooked with canned corn beef, and by the end of that job, Tony never wanted to see a can of corned beef again.

They finished their meal, and Tony looked at Alfonso, "how many guys are you concerned about?"

"Alfonso said, three people, Adam, the cook's helper, and two other fellows working in the field."

Tony looked at Alfonso, "I think I might have an idea. Are you sure the rest of the crew will come back?"

Alfonso nodded, "Yes."

"I was thinking about a midterm bonus. Maybe we should give the crew 50% now and 50% when they return in the New Year."

Alfonso thought for a minute, "That could work."

"Great, let's sleep on that tonight Tony casually said. "So the Camp will be closed on December 21 and reopen on January 5. Let's see what we can do. I don't like leaving the camp unattended for a long time. So let's see if we can find another option. I have an idea that could be beneficial to us all."

Alfonso questioned Tony, "Tony, when will you head south."

"I am flying out the morning of December 23rd."

Alphonso had numerous thoughts going through his head. First, Tony would probably like it if Alfonso volunteered to stay and take care of the camp. Second, Alfonso knew Tony did not celebrate Christmas. In fact, he knew Tony disliked this time of the year and everything that goes with it.

Tony looked at Alfonso and knew what he was thinking. "Alfonso, the fellows who go home at Christmas will be back. Am I right in making that assumption?"

"Yes," stated Alfonso.

Okay, let me tell you about my plan, and we will see if it will work. "Let's take the three fellows with nowhere to go. Send them to Thundering Waters for the nights of the 22nd through the 25th. What are you doing during this time frame."

Alfonso thought, "Nothing, really. I was just going to the city."

"Okay, can I include you in my plan?"

"Yes, by all means," Alphonso wondered what he was getting into.

"You know I don't like this time of the year. It's just a waste of money. More and more people are picking my pockets for freebies. Everyone wants something for nothing. I don't know how I got conned into this soup kitchen fiasco. But I did, and I am a man of my word, so I will provide some help. I must be off my rocker, though. So I'm going to tell you a little story. I have been in the city for a while now. One night, while walking, I came across a soup kitchen needing some help. So I have helped financially, already purchasing groceries and other needed goods. I have even worked serving patrons relying on this place for a warm meal and conversation. I found out they are short of volunteers, especially on Christmas Eve and Christmas Day. So, I'm looking for volunteers in the soup kitchen for those four nights. For their time, I will pay for their hotel and meals while they are in town. It will be a win for us. You will get your crew back for start-up in January. The camp won't be idle for long; hopefully, the crew will stay out of trouble.

It's only a short walk from the hotel to the soup kitchen. But for this generosity, I expect they will work as volunteers in the soup kitchen for those four nights. We need them for the soup kitchen. This also protects us; the guys will return to camp when it's time. So I'm not doing this to be a nice guy. But, unfortunately, most volunteers will be at home celebrating this ridiculous holiday."

Alfonso listened intently to what Tony was saying. Tony continued, not wanting to get into how he found this kitchen, the stars drawing him to the location. But, Tony thought, Alfonso did not need an explanation now, maybe later.

We will meet tomorrow just after breakfast before they go to work.
Alfonso thought this sounded interesting. He had no family and nowhere to go. So, he will keep the proposition in mind.

Tony replied, "I'm not a soul looking for redemption. This venture will supply a great tax write-off. If it's done right, the company could get the majority of that money back, so that's a win-win situation for us. The men can return to camp early, then we wouldn't have such an extended shutdown. So what do you think."

"Yes, this plan could work. Let me talk to the men after you leave."

"Okay, but I will bring the subject up when I have coffee with Adam in the morning."

Tony thought, "Alfonso, I have another question for you."

"Ask away."

Tony looked at him and said, "Do you know what happened to Adam."

Alfonso replied, "I asked him about what happened, and he said a few years back, he was working with some guys on a claim north of here. They went into town for the weekend, and from what I gathered, Adam got into a snowmobile accident. I heard that he had his leg amputated at the hospital."

"I see. It's no wonder he's hiding it from me.

Tony looked at Alphonso, "Must be time to check out the dessert counter." Tony got up and picked a piece of Key Lime pie, one of Tony's favorites. It won't be long now. Then, he will be on a plane heading south to a warm beach where Key Lime pie is a staple of life.

Tony and Alfonso spent the rest of the evening discussing the plans. What would be done and accomplished when the men returned from the holiday break. Tony told Alfonso he would leave in the morning after breakfast. Tony finished up and headed back to his room, marveling at the sky glistening with stars shining from everywhere. To the east, he could see the two stars that seemed to be calling his name nowhere near as bright as they were. Beckoning him to come back into the fold of believers. To continue on this adventure and welcome Christmas back into his heart. Tony shook his head. Time to break the funk he was in. It helped him, cleared his head, and walked to his camp trailer. Just before going inside, he looked one more time at the stars. They were still there, but the luster was definitely dying out. Enough of this nonsense, Tony thought and went in, crashed for the evening.

39

The following day, the crews headed out to the work area. Tony told them to have a pleasant time wherever they ended up for this little break in the work schedule. He never used the phrase, have a Merry Christmas, since that fateful night when his parents were taken from him so many years ago. Went over to the counter and got a coffee. Looked at Adam and said, "When you're done, let's chat."

Adam knew there was no getting away from it. Tony was tenacious when he wanted something. So he looked at Tony and said, "Okay, be over in a few minutes."

So Tony nodded his head and proceeded to go and sit at a table.
In a few minutes, Adam hobbled over, sat down, and looked at Tony.

"You still look like something the cat dragged in," Adam commented.

Tony chuckled and replied, "Well, young fella, you're not looking much better."

Adam laughed heartily, "I guess you're right."

"You're a cook helper now, a far cry from the guy I used to know. What the heck happened to you.

When you left me, you were heading north, looking for that elusive gold mine. I kept track of you for a bit, and then you disappeared."

"I moved around a lot," always found work but nothing worthwhile. So how did your venture turn out at Dark Waters?"

"Still working on it," Tony replied a little white lie for now. "Not sure where it's heading, do have some interested parties."

Adam nodded, looking at Tony. "I've had a hard time finding work, so I'm hoping this venture here will pay off." Adam continued to speak. As I said, I moved around a lot. Couldn't find anything that struck my fancy. At one time, I thought about tracking you down to see if you had anything exciting."

"What happened to your leg," Tony asked.

Adam replied, "A few years back, I worked outside a small northern town. The crew and I were at the bar one-night having drinks. It was a Friday night; they were having snowmachine races the next day, and I overheard a guy saying nobody would beat him on his sled. Being the type of guy I am, I moved on to where he was sitting and made him a proposition. I will put two hundred up for a private race with you, just the two of us on the track. You do the same, and we'll see what happens. We will do three laps around the course.

The guy looked at me and said this would be the easiest and fastest two hundred I've ever made. I had a buddy that I was working with. He had a brand new powerful sled. I asked if I could use it for the race, and he said sure, but we split the winnings fifty-fifty each. I looked at the fellow and said, "OK, you're on."

The next day was sunny, and the temperature was just right. We got to the track early enough so we could watch the races. This guy knew what he was doing and always stayed second or third. Still, on that last lap, he would move to the inside and shoot up the gap, passing everyone. After that, he was free and clear to the finish line. Watched him three times, and he used that trademark move every time. So, I thought I got this figured out now. The plan was that on the last lap, I would have to ensure that I stayed tight to the inside on the remaining curve. The first two laps went like clockwork.

I was out in front and thought I had it. We came into the final lap, and I could see that sled coming up fast on me. If you want to go by me, it will be on the outside. I lost my concentration for a second, and I slipped outside. We hit the corner, and he shot by me just as I tried to maneuver my sled back in tight to the corner. Little did I know that he was just toying with me. So, I leaned in to try and cut him off, had my leg dangling outside the footrest, and we bumped together. The next thing I knew, he was by me, and my boot was dangling. That's all I remember. I was told that my foot was severed just above the ankle. I still didn't know what had happened, but my leg hurt, my machine quit, and I fell off. I was being loaded into the ambulance, and I was asked if I knew what had happened. Off to the hospital we went. I was later told they tried everything but could not save my foot. They did a clean amputation. So when I healed and needed a job, the only thing I could do was become a cook helper, which was a lot less moving around. I knew working in the field was not an option."

Tony looked at Adam and said, "You're a mining engineer. So why didn't you go and look and see if you can find work doing that?"

Adam replied, "I did, but the industry had taken a downturn, and no one was hiring, especially a guy with a gimp leg. So, after the summer, I saw this job and applied, and Alfonso hired me. It's good I still get to be out in the bush. It's not perfect, but it's not the worst."

Tony looked at Adam and asked, "Have you given up looking for work as a mining engineer. It might be a little easier and less stressful on your leg.

Adam replied, "No, not at all, just waiting for the market to pick up; then I will look around to see what I can find."

"Didn't you tell me you had a special girl at one time? Whatever happened to her."

"I did. We were going to be forever, but through time, work, and traveling, we lost track of each other. So then we went our own separate ways. Last I heard, she married and settled in Thundering Waters."

"Are you coming to Thundering Waters for winter break?"

"Yes, there are three of us. But, unfortunately, we don't have a family, so we considered going to town."

Tony looked at Adam, "I have to talk to Alfonso, and I think we will need someone to watch the camp for the downtime. I was wondering if you and your amigos might be interested in this. Head to Thundering Waters On December 22nd, then head back to camp on the morning of the 26th to keep the home fires burning.

"That sounds like a great idea," replied Adam.

"There is a provision for this. I found a soup kitchen on my walks around Thundering Waters and have been helping them. This place is run by Annabel Heaven and her husband, Harry. They need some help feeding the lost souls over the holiday. I inquired what they would do on Christmas Eve and Christmas Day. She told me that they would probably be closed. The problem is they are short of volunteers, not patrons. I thought this could be a win-win for us and the soup kitchen. The company will pick up your rooms and food within reason. All you guys have to do is be there for the soup kitchen. Volunteer for those four days."

Adam looked at Tony, "where are you going to be."

"Hopefully, someplace warm, sitting on a friendly beach.

"Oh, when do you need the answer."

"As soon as possible, Adam, could you talk to the other guys and see if they would be willing to do this. You can then let Alfonso know, and he could pass the message on to me. If it's positive, I can make some arrangements with the hotel. Also, talk to Annabel to let her know she has help for those days if she wants it."

"Sounds good, "Adam said he would let Alfonso know as quickly as possible. My look at the time we sat and chatted the whole morning away. Better let you get back to work, and I better go and say goodbye to Alfonso and head back to Thundering Waters.

"When are you heading South," Adam queried.

"On the morning of the 23rd."

"OK, hopefully, we'll bump into each other again. Please be careful."

"I will," replied Tony as he stood, shook Adam's hand, and headed out the door. Tony strolled to Alfonso's office to give him the bonus checks for the crew. Fifty percent now and the remainder when they return from the Christmas break. "Alfonso, I'm going to head out now and return to Thundering Waters. I've talked to Adam about watching the camp with the other two guys. He thought it was a good idea and told him about coming into town for four nights and doing a particular job for the company and me. They will let you know what their thoughts are. Once you find out, let me know. Just call me at the hotel. If I'm not in, just leave a message. Yes, they will do it, or no, they're not interested. Keep the bonus checks until they leave camp for the break."

"Perfect," Alfonso replied, "are you heading out now."

"Yes," he shook Alfonso's hand and wished him happy holidays.

Alfonso looked at Tony, "You too, my friend, be careful. Have a good time on that sunny beach."

"I will," replied Tony as he headed out the door.

40

Tony climbed into the truck and headed back to Thundering Waters, driving along the lake shore, looking out to see the vastness of the big lake, cold and forbidding. A lake that very seldom froze over. On the way back, Tony thought about what had happened last week and the future. No one can answer that. Dam those stars for creating havoc on his simple life. Christmas is not needed. Who cares about this ridiculous time of the year? Not me, that's for sure. Tony thought, what kind of a savior of mankind, leaving these lost souls looking for a meal, a spot to stay warm. Look what this so-called savior did to him on that night many years ago. There was no rejoicing in Tony's heart and soul. All that remained was sadness, rage, and hate. His whole life had changed. In a matter of seconds, the last picture in his mind was his mom and dad's look of horror on their faces. They knew the end was happening. There were no goodbyes, just the sounds of pain and mangled metal; these were the sounds he remembered on his birthday. They will stay with him, and he will never forget, no rejoicing on his plate. Finally, Thundering Waters is only a couple miles away. Go out, grab a quick bite, or have room service; why not? He could afford it.

As he was parking, it was time to finish what he had started. But there will be no more giving. So, it was time to cut and run. This Christmas spirit has got to be put back into the bottom of the wishing bottle and left there.

Tony gave the keys to the desk agent, and she said she would take care of getting the truck back to the rental company. Tony got to his room. He was exhausted too much thinking on the way back. Stripped down, took a hot shower, and had a cheeseburger. Then, to bed, sleep came quickly. No dreams, no thoughts, just a good sleep.

41

In the morning, Tony thought, I will be on a plane heading south in a few days.

Thinking about yesterday's drive, some thoughts went through Tony's mind. First, Tony thought moving to Thundering Waters would suit the company, and the location would be great. Second, restoring the old church would be a positive move. Third, letting the soup kitchen stay until March would be another positive move. Finally, helping Joan, her family, Adam, and the camp crews would be a positive move, making Tony think he is somewhat of an angelic fellow. Tony chuckled; a few good deeds will make me feel good. So, what's on the agenda today? First, head to Mitch's Renovations to see what kind of a plan she has devised. Then, a visit to Giuseppe's Italian Market was in order. After that, stop at the bank for a quick chat with Eric Luckseno. As he was leaving, Tony caught a glimpse of himself in the mirror and thought he better look for a barber shop as well. The comment from Adam saying Tony looked like a lost soul made him feel he should clean up a bit. Then, off to Vi's Tavern to meet Joan and her kids for supper.

She was a charming person, just down on her luck. Tony thought it would be nice for the kids to eat away from the soup kitchen, and having company during the evening meal would be nice.

Thought it was always lovely to meet other people, but at this time of the year, Tony wished to be alone; why did he ask her out in the first place. It sure wasn't loneliness; he's been doing this all his life. Then he thought about those two stars following him in his every move. They were creating uncertainty in his lifestyle; why him? He will never know. He just knew they were going to be a pain in his lifestyle.

42

After breakfast, Tony stepped onto the street and noticed it had warmed up. Main Street was quiet. Not an abundance of shoppers yet. Tony walked down the street, turned left, and headed toward Mitchell's shop. Ten minutes later, he walked into the door. She was in the same spot as the other day when she looked up and saw Tony. He still looked like a bum, but appearances don't tell the whole story. Tony looked at Mitch. Did you have any breakthroughs on the weekend on the project we discussed?

Mitch looked at Tony, "Let's go to my office. I have a bunch of sketches for you to look at."

"Right, let's do it." Tony liked the general layout: plenty of office space, a reception area, and a great boardroom. Washrooms in the back and a small kitchen area. Tony asked Mitch, "What about the steeple? Got any ideas?".

"Not yet. We will leave it as is for now."

Tony looked at Mitch, OK, I'll sleep on it for the next few days, see what I can come up with. So that brings me to the question: When could you start on this project."

'Well, probably right after the New Year. Have you decided on a budget figure yet?"

"Well, I'm thinking around one hundred thousand. I'm hoping that will be on the high side. I will set up an account with you as the primary contact after me. It will be at the Royal Blue Bank; you'll have to go in and sign some papers."

"Sounds good," Mitch commented.

Tony got up, shook Mitch's hand, and said, "Great, have a wonderful day."

Tony left and decided it was an excellent time to have a quick visit with Guiseppe and Angelina. Tony arrived at the market, and both Guiseppe and Angelina were busy.

"Good afternoon," Tony called out, "how are things progressing? Do you need more financing, or is everything okay now?"

Angelina answered; Tony knew she was the planner of this little venture. "Everything is looking good."

"Great," Tony replied. "I'm going to the bank in a bit; maybe I will put another couple of thousand into your account."

"That would be wonderful," replied Guiseppe, even though he got the look from Angelina stating it wasn't needed.

"Okay, I'm off," replied Tony. "Have a good afternoon."

Tony stepped out and headed to the bank.

Tony saw Eric waiting for him as he stepped through the bank doors.

Eric looked at Tony and commented, "How do you do."

"Feeling very well, thanks for asking." Are the documents ready for my signature,"

"Yes, all the documents requiring your signature are ready to be signed. Some are in the name of Black Wolf Reality, a subsidiary company of The Eagle Mining and Prospecting Company. The funds will be transferred into the respective accounts this afternoon.

"Great, now I must decide what to do with the old church. Remember, when Annabel comes in this afternoon, she signs the lease until the end of March. So we must ensure that the church ownership can not be traced back to me."

"Not a problem. What else do we need to discuss."

"I also need you to post Fifty Thousand into my account for Alfonso. He uses this account for daily expenses on the project east of town. Also, transfer another two thousand into the account for the Italian Market. Can you set up a new account under the Black Wolf Reality Company? Then, place one hundred thousand dollars into this account for Mitch's Renovations. I gave her the contract to start the renovations in the New Year. She will be in to sign the papers. That's all I have for today."

Eric commented, "OK, I will take care of that at the same time this afternoon when I make the other transfers."

"Well, I guess that's it for now, "I will see you in a couple of days."

Tony got up, slipped his coat on, and strolled out the office door. All the financial areas were taken care of. He can fly off to warmer climates without worrying about all the lost souls he's trying to help. But then a thought crossed his mind from the other side of his brain, asking him what you are trying to do. Tony did not have an answer to that question.

45

Tony headed west with the snow crunching underfoot. It was time to get cleaned up a bit and look a little more professional, so to speak. He was looking for a barbershop that he had visited years ago. The shoppers were out in full force. Tony went by Vi's Tavern, and there was a small building with a sign, Fernando's Barbershop.

Tony walked in; there were three chairs in a row, all red and white.

An older gentleman looked at Tony, "Can we help you.

Tony looked around; the place was full of patrons yammering about anything and everything. The scent of barbershop life returned to Tony. Clipper oil with a strong odor of talc powder and cigarette smoke. Tony knew he was in the right place. "Well, as you can see, I need a trim, and the beard has to go."

The barber looked at Tony, "Well, you have come to the right place. I am called Fernando De Luca Rizzo, Fernie for short, artist extraordinaire, and you are?"

"Antonio Barbossa."

OK, let's get you seated and see what kind of magic we can impact on you. Fernando took Tony to the sink and had him bend almost in two so he could wash his hair. With that job complete, he took Tony back to his chair, where the magic was about to begin. Fernando took his scissors, working his magic on his hair with lightning speed. Did this and that, and the haircut was complete, longish, but very stylish. Next up was the scraggly beard. The scissors did their job again, cutting the longish hair and getting ready for the straight razor. Fernando then put a hot towel on his face. This opened up the pores, softened the skin, and smoothed out the hair, ready for the straight razor.

Next, Fernando applied shaving cream with a brush and bowel, the smell not overpowering but clean. Then he finished with the straight razor. In a matter of minutes, Tony could see his clean face. Once again, a hot towel was applied to clean the soap residue from his face. The final act of completing this transformation was to liberally splash some Yves St. Laurent on his face. This had a cooling effect on his skin, and it felt terrific. Finally, Tony looked in the mirror, and a new man was looking back at him. A rugged wind-burnt face but quite a handsome fellow, Tony thought to himself. This was a pampering he had not allowed himself ever. Tony reminded himself we'll have to do this more often.

After paying, Tony bid Fernando goodbye.

Leaving the barbershop, he returned to his hotel room to change and get ready to meet with Joan and her two kids.

Tony wondered why Joan had grown on him. He really wanted more background on Joan. Tony wondered if she would be a good fit to run the finances for the new ventures he had set up with Eric from the bank. His mining company, the new reality company, and the Lost Soul charity.

Ready to go, Tony bundled up and exited the hotel. Made his way to Vi's Tavern. He arrived with fifteen minutes to spare before Joan and her kids arrived at this unique establishment.

Tony stepped into the tavern, the smells making his pallet jump. The smell lifted his spirits to a new high. It smelt like Sunday at home so many years ago.

Vi came out from the kitchen and looked directly at Tony. She had difficulty placing him with his haircut and the cleaner look. She got closer, and then she realized who it was.

"Oh, you again, you look more respectful today. Whata you want?" asked Vi.

Tony looked at her and said, "I need a table for four people, two adults and two children. I'm having dinner with a wonderful lady with her family."

She looked at Tony, "You better be on the up and up; otherwise, I'm gonna makea trouble for you."

"Yes, everything is on the up and up,"

"Well, come on with me. Here is a nice place by the window," stated Vi.

"This will be fine."

Vi looked at Tony repeatedly, "You clean up pretty good."

"Thank you."

Vi commented, "I made a new batch of sauce this morning; that's why the place smell a so good."

"Yes," Tony replied, looking at Vi. "How are the meatballs."

Vi looked at Tony with a devious smile; "they are perfect, made a fresh from yesterday."

"Good," the kids said they would like spaghetti and meatballs. I told them I knew of a great place that makes the best spaghetti and meatballs I have ever tasted. So you're not going let me down, are you?"

Vi looked at Tony; "not a chance I make abest spaghetti and meatballs in the city. You like I bring you a glass of Vino today?"

"No thanks, but I will have a beer and a glass."

"OK, I'll bring you a beer and glass."

Tony sat quietly, pondering what is the end game here. Something in the air keeps pushing him to accept Christmas and be nice simultaneously. It's been a long time since he felt like this. So he thought, we'll keep riding this horse until he throws me to the ground.

A little while later, Joan and her two children came in; they saw Tony and meandered over to the table.

Joan looked at Tony, "I almost didn't recognize you; you have been busy cleaning up."

Tony looked at Joan; "sit down, please; thanks for noticing. I feel like a new man. I am pleased you took me up on my invitation. It will be nice to have someone to enjoy a meal with."

Just then, Vi appeared with Tony's beer, noticed the woman with the kids looking over, and thought they didn't look like trouble.

Vi then asked, "How are you this evening? What can I bring you to drink."

Joan replied, "She would have coke, for the kids, orange soda if that was possible. Thank you."

"I will be right back with the drinks, but before I go, I will leave the menus for you. My specialty today is the best spaghetti and meatballs in the city; anyway, I will get drinks now." Vi returned ten minutes later with the drinks. Tony had ordered a plate full of bruschetta for everyone to munch on.

Vi asked, "OK, now what does everyone want to eat."

Tony looked at Vi, "I will have your special spaghetti and meatballs."

Joan replied, "I will have the same thing, and so will the children."

"Perfect, I go get the order in and tell the chef to make his specialty for a bunch of nicea people."

Tony smiled as he knew there was no chef in the kitchen. Instead, Vi was the chief cook, bottle washer, and number one server, running a one-woman show.

Tony, Joan, and the kids sat munching on the bruschetta Vi had put on the table. They all commented on how good it was.

Tony looked at Joan. So, the last we chatted, you told me you had some accounting background.

Joan was taken aback by the question. What was going on? She certainly did not want to be interrogated for a free meal. Oh well, she thought, let's just see where this goes.

"Yes," she said, "I was a senior accountant at my last job. I would be there now, except I had to give notice when my husband got sick. Then, the bottom fell out of the market, and my previous company had some financial problems. Tony knew all this information. So he was double-checking that Joan would be a perfect fit for what he had in mind.

Thinking to himself, Joan, Adam, and Annabel would make a formidable team. Annabel would care for the charity, Adam would do the mining, and Joan would oversee the financing.

Vi showed up with the meals, and the kids dug in with fierce appetites. Joan was tentatively poking at her dinner. She thought something didn't add up with this fellow; she was unsure what.

Meal complete dessert was had, and it was time to pay the bill and head out. Vi slipped Tony the bill for the meal. Joan and the kids got up and left the table, and Tony placed the money and a sizable tip under his plate.

Tony slipped his parka on and met Joan and the kids outside.

Joan and the children said, "Thank you for the wonderful meal."

"Would you like to go for a walk?"

No, thank you. It was time to head home, "but thank you for the invitation."

"Are you going to be at the soup kitchen in the next few nights?"

"Yes, we will be there, as she still had difficulty making ends meet."

"Great, I will see you there."

Joan and her kids went on their way, and Tony was on his way back to his room.

47

Thinking soon, he would have to let people know his plans. Maybe everyone else might not want to be involved in his grandiose idea. He assumed everyone would be okay and share his passion with him.

Walking back to the hotel, Tony wondered why and how this happened. If there is a heaven, my mom and his dad are there, and you can bet they have something to do with the strangeness in his life.

It was early evening, and Tony decided to walk down Main Street. He left Vi's and was standing on main street within five minutes. The hustle and bustle seemed everywhere, with a carnival type of atmosphere. Music could be heard, and people were hustling and clutching bags of purchased goods.

A strange thought came over Tony. This was a time of the season to remember Christ's birthday. Over time, the remembrance and goodwill towards men have been replaced with commercializing and partying. From what Tony could see, charity and goodwill towards mankind could no longer be found. It's no wonder the soup kitchen was left to its demise only blocks from here. Tony watched the hustle and bustle and decided to call it a night. He returned to his hotel, said good evening to the desk clerk, and went to his room. Had a hot shower to shake the chill that had overcome him. Then, headed to bed. A fitful sleep followed dreams about souls in the soup kitchen and what he could do.

48

Tony opened his eyes after a fitful sleep and decided it was time to get up. He walked to the bathroom and looked at himself in the mirror. It is time to shower, shave, and prepare for the day's adventures. Grabbing his coat, he looked outside and saw the smoke from the furnaces on the other buildings slowly creeping up to the sky. Decided it was a good morning for a walk in the brisk morning air. Maybe it would clear his head. The thoughts he was having were neither rational nor irrational. He was not sure what the heck he was doing.

Heading south towards the big lake, decided to walk along the lakeshore. After a few minutes, there was a bench; Tony sat down and looked out at the frozen wasteland, pondering life or what was to become of life.

After sitting for a while, he decided it was time for breakfast and to develop a new plan revolving around him. No one else is saving the world, so why should I. Let's just save Tony and his cash.

Tony stopped at a little hole-in-the-wall restaurant and had coffee and breakfast; nagging thoughts kept extending in his mind. Thought to himself, why did he buy the church and devise ridiculous plans to try and save the world. This is not in his nature. He hated Christmas, hated his birthday.

All he remembered was that night so many years ago when his life changed forever. With each bite, his thoughts were saying one thing, and his heart was saying something different. Those dam stars would be the end of him. He was now shocked by what he had almost tied himself into. The soup kitchen and the old church are a liability now. Still, he should be able to offload the Church for a tidy profit when the renovations are complete. Breakfast was finished; he knew what he had to do. Tomorrow morning, he would be on a plane to a warm beach far away from here. It will be time for rest and relaxation. He decided he would stay south at least till the end of January. When he flew back to Thundering Waters, it would be time to check on the church renovations. Then, head east of Thundering Waters to check on his latest ventures. He would do some work while down south, research an old mine that was closed down to see if there would be any viability to bring the area back to life. This area was only about 100 miles away from his current interests.

In his mind, Tony had a plan in place. First, stop at Mitch's Reno's to see how the projects were coming. Second, go to the Italian grocery store and chat with Angelina and Giuseppe to ensure they have the food ordered and have enough cash to pay their bills. The third stop is the bank stop and chat with Eric Luckseno to ensure accounts are set up. Finally, have a bite to eat at the tavern and say goodbye to Vi. Then, off to the soup kitchen to give Annabel the bad news. Also, remember to remind the crew, Eric, Angelina, Giuseppe, and Mitch, the next few nights that they will be helping out at the soup kitchen if possible.

49

Tony walked down the street, headed for Mitchell's restoration. As he walked in, he saw Mitch working furiously on a drawing.

"Hello, there; how are we doing."

Mitch looked up from the drawing, "everything is coming together."

"That's great."

She looked at him and said, "I'm not sure about the steeple just yet; I'm working on the bones first."

"Sounds great; my only comment is let's make sure we just concentrate on the main floor, turning it into office space as previously discussed. But, first, we must ensure the electrical and plumbing are up to standard."

Mitch had a puzzled look on her face and commented, "Are we about to change plans now."

Tony looked at her and replied, "Yes, I would like all renovations completed early in the spring. After that, I want to put the building on the market. It no longer fits my plans. Will the budget we talked about still work?"

"Yes, it will."

"Great he said. The accounts with Royal Blue Bank are set up. You will have signing authority on the account. With that, I bid you goodbye. I'm heading south tomorrow morning and won't return until the end of January."

Mitch looked at him and wanted to ask why the change of plans but thought better of it. Instead, she looked at Tony and replied, "I can start right after the holiday if that's ok."

"That would be fine."

She glanced at Tony and said, "Goodbye, Merry Christmas; we will see you in January."

Tony looked over his shoulder, "Goodbye. Oh, one other thing: I'm hoping I can count on you to help in the soup kitchen the next few nights."

"Yes, I will be there," stated Mitch.

50

Tony left the shop and headed for the Italian Market. Upon arriving, he saw Angelina sitting behind the counter. Then he saw Joe muttering, moving to and fro in the store. Angelina wanted some of the Christmas products moved to the front of the store, with a better chance of selling them. Giuseppe continued muttering that he would move it wherever Angelina wanted it. However, this process created extra work for him but made Angelina happy.

She acknowledged Tony, "Hello, how are you doing."

Tony replied, "Fine," spotted Joe, and told Angelina, "I need to have a quick conversation with you both."

"Joe looked up from what he was doing. Ciao Antonio, how are you? I'm fine, so good to see you."

Tony looked at Joe. "Can we have a quick conversation between the three of us? This won't take long; where do you suggest."

"The front of the store would be fine; you like a coffee replied Giuseppe."

"Yes, that would be great."

Tony got his coffee and looked at both Joe and Angelina. "Have you turned in the extra order for the soup kitchen Tony asked?"

"Yes," replied Angelina, "everything will be here tomorrow. We will have it covered with our supplies if anything is shorted. Everything should go as planned. The order is paid as per your instructions. I was going to bring the bills to the bank tomorrow for Mr. Luckseno. We will deliver all the goods to Mrs. Heaven tomorrow."

Tony looked at Angelina, "If they don't have room for everything, will you be able to store the goods for them."

"Yes, that will not be a problem."

Tony looked at them both with sadness in his eyes, "Are you going to be at the kitchen tomorrow night and the next night, the 23rd and the 24th. The 23rd is to help prepare everything, while the 24th is to feed the lost souls. I won't be there. I'm on my way to Mexico in the morning. I hope to sit on the beach far away from here by tomorrow afternoon. I have done enough, and now it's time for Tony. Now it's time to move on, so with everything in order, I will say goodbye. I will drop in and see you when I return from the South around the end of January. Mr. Luckseno has been instructed to add more money to the account as needed. That will have to carry you until the

New Year; I will not be covering for any more supplies after the first week in January."

Angelina and Giuseppe looked at Tony. "Merry Christmas and goodbye." Angelina looked at Joe. "What is going on?"

"I don't know, but he's not happy; right now, he's lost, not knowing where he's going. So he must continue his journey and hope for happiness," stated Giuseppe.

On his way to the bank, Tony noticed Main Street's extra hustle and bustle; people were scattered to and fro spending their money on Christmas. What a waste. Tony thought this was ridiculous. Finally arriving at the bank, Tony stepped inside. Eric Luckseno was talking to the receptionist and saw Tony. He motioned him to come over so they could head to his office. Tony was glad he wanted this to be a short visit to ensure everything was in order. So they entered Eric's office, and Tony replied, "Let's get down to business." "Number one, no extensions on the soup kitchen; when the lease ends at the end of March, I want them gone."

"Number two is the account set up for Mitch to renovate the old church building. She will start drawing funds in the New Year."

"I need a cheque for Adam Watson for one hundred thousand dollars. I promised him when I first met him that if the property he helped me with ever bore fruit, I would not forget him. So you can give him his funds on January 3rd."

The last thing is to put another two thousand in Joe and Angelina's account for the Italian Market. This should cover them until the first week in January for the required groceries. "That's all I have, Eric. Do you need anything?"

"Just one thing," Eric responded, "what happened to the plan for the soup kitchen? Not really any of my business. You can change your mind if you wish, but I thought you would be the philanthropist to help them."

"I have thought about it and concluded it's time for Tony. Before I came along, there was no one to help them. I thought I could do it but decided no, it's Tony's time. So, it's time for me to cut and run. It's time for Tony to take care of Tony."

"Ok," I will get what we have discussed in motion."

Tony looked at Eric, "Once the old church renovations are complete in the spring. Then, the church will be sold, and I should make a tidy profit."

"Well, goodbye, my friend. I will see you in the New Year."

"Ok, I assume you will not be helping on Christmas Eve at the kitchen."

"Yes, you have presumed right," Tony looked at Eric, "I will be on the beach in Mexico and relaxing with a cool drink. We will see you when I get back." By the way, I told Annabel Heaven that you would be there to help out. I hope that's still true."

As he walked out the door, Tony heard Eric say, "Yes, I will be there; goodbye and Merry Christmas."

52

Tony stepped out and looked up and down the street; the shoppers were out in full force, getting that last-minute trinket they thought they needed to make someone happy. Tony stopped briefly. Thinking back to when he was a child. Christmas was a family affair; there were always small gifts to be had, but not to the extent of what was happening now. This was not how Christmas should be; his parents taught him a different version that disappeared many years ago. Tony started walking in the brisk evening air, thinking it was time for a quick meal and then going to the soup kitchen to give Annabel the bad news.

Tony arrived at the tavern and stepped in; the smell of the sauce and other delights made Tony even hungrier than he thought was possible. Tony sat, not waiting to be seated, just to see if he could get a reaction from Vi. Finally, he looked up from what he was reading, and Vi made her way to where he was sitting.

" Itsa you; you still donoa how to read; what's that paper for."

"Good evening; how are you tonight? " Tony countered. I see you're as pleasant as ever; I don't know why I come here to eat just to be insulted by you. However, I'm here now, so I might as well order; I will have gnocchi, Italian sausage, and a cold beer. Do you think you can handle that?"

"Okay, I'ma go in the kitchen makea you meal." You're gona be here for Christmas. I'm gonna be closed that day."

"No, I am heading south tomorrow morning and won't return till the end of January."

"Oh, that's gona be a nice trip. I'ma hope you have a gooda time," she replied as she headed off to the kitchen.

Tony sat quietly, reading the paper until his meal arrived.

The meal showed up, and the smell made him feel like he had just walked inside a ravenous pit of delight; he was starving. Tony ate slowly, enjoying every last morsel on his plate. Complete Tony paid his bill and said goodbye to Vi. Although he heard Vi wish him a Merry Christmas on the way out the door, he continued without acknowledging her greeting.

Vi thought to herself she was right. He was a rude man.

53

Tony made his way to the church; on his way, he could see those two dam stars shining down. Thought to himself, glad I came to my senses when I did. Whatever prompted me to believe he could save these lost souls. Yes, they needed help. Go to the churches, go to the governments they could help. Who was there to help me all those years ago. Lived in an orphanage to fend for himself. One thing, he was alone; there was no one, just him, and if he wanted a better life, it would be up to him to achieve his dreams without help from anyone else. He arrived at the door, looked up at the sky, and saw those dam stars haunting him since the day he left camp. They were no longer as bright as they had been. Finally, he was extinguishing the save-the-world thoughts from his mind.

Tony stepped through the door and walked into the soup kitchen; he could not believe what had happened in the days since he first entered. He stepped into the open and saw Annabel barking orders to the men who volunteered under Tony's direction. Could see Adam hobbling along but smiling from ear to ear. He seemed very happy, almost like his life had changed. Tony stepped in and said hello to everyone, spotted Annabel, and strode over to where she was.

He commented, "It looks like the day is going smoothly."

"Yes, Joan and the kids will be in later. I think we will have a job for them."

"That's great, the ordered food will be delivered tomorrow. If you run short of room, Angelina said they can store it at the store until needed."

"That is wonderful," Annabel commented, "we will have enough food to carry us through till the New Year. So I suppose I have to thank you for the extra food."

"No thanks required. I was glad I was able to do a little something." Thinking Tony knew nothing else needed to be said. He was packed and ready to go in the morning, flying out on his way south to a warm beach. It's time to enjoy his time. At least, that's what was on his mind. Tony looked at Annabel, "We have to chat before the night is over."

Annabel looked over and replied, "I knew this was coming."

"What are you talking about," Tony thought Annabel knew what was coming.

"About you not going to be here to help after tonight."

She was partly right. Tony knew he had to talk with Annabel, which would be difficult. So Tony was ready to start the conversation with Annabel, and Joan and her two kids came in and sauntered over to where Tony and Annabel were chatting.

54

Joan looked at Annabel and inquired, "Where would you like us to be tonight? We're going to work for our meal."

"Just go over and see that fella with the red hair and the big beard. He will explain what he needs help with."

Joan looked over, and a huge smile and a look of bewilderment came over her face.

Tony immediately noticed that and commented, "Joan, what's wrong? Looks like you've just seen a ghost."

Joan looked at Tony, "I think I have. I don't believe my eyes, that fellow. His name is Adam Watson, if I remember correctly."

Tony looked at her, "I'm not sure. I think I heard some of the other fellows called him Adam."

Joan looked at Tony, "If that is Adam Watson, we know each other. He was my high school sweetheart; actually, he was more than that. We made plans for life after high school. But it wasn't in the cards. He went his way to get his engineering degree, and I went my way to get my accounting designation. At first, we kept in touch and would try to get together at every chance. We kept in touch for a while, and as time passed, we drifted apart. Finally, I met my husband, got together with Adam one last time, and said goodbye. Adam was understanding, or so I thought. The last I heard about him was that he was off chasing rainbows in the form of gold mines. The rest is history; Adam went his way, and I went mine."

55

"I must say excuse me and go over and say hello." So Joan and her kids made their way over to where Adam was. He had his back to her when she came up and said, "Excuse me, but I'm here to help you along with my two children. I was told to come and see you, and you would steer us in the right direction."

Adam heard that voice and did not move. He knew who it was but could not believe his ears and was afraid to turn around. What is she doing here? Adam thought, must be a high society volunteer here with her kids, trying to teach them that it's okay to help the downtrodden, especially at this time of the year. Adam did not want to make a move with his bum leg, afraid she would feel sorry for him.

Joan waited, and no sound came from Adam's lips. "Excuse me, sir, but did you not hear what I said? We are here to help you; what would you like us to do."

"I heard you; I'm not deaf, you know," as he slowly turned around, unsure what to expect.

Their eyes met, and years of memories flashed by. Years of being on the run trying to fill the void of loneliness. "How are you, Joan? I'm sorry you caught me at this moment in my life."

"What moment are you talking about," Joan asked.

'At this moment, I am volunteering here with a bum leg. Being one of the lost souls, a far cry from what we would achieve in our youth. Look at you; I'm surprised to see you here volunteering. Is it your way of giving back to people in need?"

'Never noticed the leg. You have hardly moved from the time we started chatting. But life is not always what it seems. We will have to have coffee after helping and catch up on life. Right now, we have work to do."

"Yes," Adam replied. The workstation was set up just like at camp. Adam knew he could cover ninety percent of the serving line without moving too much, making it much easier on his leg. Positioning the kids at the end of the serving line. Explained to them what their jobs would entail. Johnny and Lucy were like sponges soaking it all in. Joan will start the serving line, handing out the plates, utensils, coffee and soup, and anything else the lost souls might require. Joan thought it felt good to be on this side of the line helping. The children were having a great time. Adam seemed to be enjoying himself.

56

Everyone was in position just in time. Annabel came by and told them the doors were about to open. Are we ready?

The doors opened, and the lost souls ventured in; all they sought was a place to sit in the warmth, a hot cup of coffee, and a hot meal.

Everything went off like clockwork. The new help that Tony supplied from the camp. Really knew what they were doing. Just over an hour ticked by, and everything was under control. Finally, Tony thought it was time to have that chat with Annabel. Tony spotted her on the other side of the room, casually walked over to where she was standing, and quietly said, "Let's find a corner so we can sit down and chat."

"Ok, let's grab a coffee."

They sat down. Looking into his coffee, Tony slowly looked up at Annabel and said, "I will start and tell you my story; if you have questions, let's save them till I'm done, please."

Annabel commented and said, "Okay, fine."

Tony started the story. "As you know, my name is Antonio Barbossa. I was born in Thundering Waters. My parents died in a terrific car crash on

Christmas Eve. We were on our way to midnight service in 1955. This church used to be our beacon of hope. Then, my life changed forever on that fateful Christmas Eve many years ago. A terrific car accident happened on that corner, and my parents were killed instantly."

"As you can see, I survived, and once I was well enough, I was sent to an orphanage. After realizing what was taken from me on this night of so-called celebration, I decided I would never celebrate my birthday or Christmas again. However, I still question what kind of a God would do that to an innocent child: rip his parents away and leave him alone."

Tony continued the story. He told Annabel he got through high school, went to university, and graduated with a geology degree with the help of some of his mentors. Then, he became a prospector and traveled all over the country studying rocks. Tony was out working for other companies. Before long, he started his own company called Eagle Mining and Prospecting Corporation. To make a long story short, finding some fascinating rocks, he staked the area and put the claims in his name. This is where he met Adam. Adam came and helped him for a couple years and then left for greener pastures. Although Tony stayed on, knowing the property was showing potential. He knew it would be a mine someday.

Tony sold the property to another Mining Company for an undisclosed amount of cash and was now set for life. With the deal closed, Tony decided he would come to Thundering Waters. Not knowing why, but felt something or someone was calling him. That morning, when he walked to the office to sign the papers, he looked up into the sky, felt like he was looking into his soul, and noticed the two stars beckoning him to follow their lead. So, he came to town to make sure the funds were deposited. I went to the other firm's office and closed out the deal. When complete, Tony decided to go for a walk. He walked towards the commercial area, which he remembered as a kid shopping with his mother. The place had not changed much, but Christmas was much more commercialized. On his walk, he realized he did not want anything to do with Christmas, his birthday, or this season. He walked the streets, and as he came to the corner, he looked, and in front of him was a dark, seemingly abandoned Avenue. Looking up at the sky, he saw the two stars, looking like he could touch them. He decided to walk down the street towards where the stars were beckoning him to come.

Before long, Tony saw the church's steeple, looked up, and saw the bright stars shining, guiding his way. Tony looked around. This was the spot where the terrible accident occurred so many years ago. It wasn't a church anymore, but a sign showed that the Lost Souls Soup Kitchen was in the basement and would open at 6:00 p.m. every night. Tony walked to the front door to see if he could open it to go in, but it was locked. He walked around the side of the building, found a door that was ajar, and crept in. The rest is history.

"That's the first time I met you. I looked around and figured you might need some extra help. But, instead, you looked at me and told me I looked like a lost soul, not someone who could help.

I assured you I could carry my weight, seeing you needed help, and figured I was free for a couple of weeks, so I offered free labor while I was in town.

After a couple of days, I noticed the church was up for sale. So I decided in a fleeting moment to buy it. So right now, I'm your landlord. At the time, I figured I would set it up so you could have a longer-term place to do your work. I'm going to be doing some renovations upstairs and was going to move my mining company here. It all started because the dam stars took hold of me like demons in the night. Making me think I was doing the right thing, saving the kitchen and the world. Then, as I was walking one night, I came to my senses. I'm not here to save the world. I made a decision. You have till the spring, then you will have to relocate. When the renovations are complete, I'm selling the building. I thought about the decision but have concluded that I have to take care of myself first.

So I will leave here and be on a flight tomorrow morning and be on a beach tomorrow afternoon. I'm sorry I didn't have better news for you. Christmas is for the fools. I thought I would make a change, but in the end, I don't know how it got this far."

Annabel looked at Tony. "That is a remarkable story; I wish it had a different outcome. I'm so sorry you feel that way. But, you must do what you must. God took care of us before you came along and will take care of us after you leave. It was a pleasure getting to know you. I hope you find the answers to your quest. I know there is more to you than meets the eye. I really do hope that you will find your answers. Goodbye and Merry Christmas, my friend." Anabel got up, left the little table, and returned to the kitchen. She didn't want Tony to see the tears in her eyes.

57

Tony got up, bundled up, and left the building. He did not want to say goodbye to anyone. Joan saw him leaving and ran after him, but it was too late. He was gone.

Joan came back and sat with Adam. As I said before, not everything is as it seems. She proceeded to tell him what had happened with her life. Adam looked at her and did the same thing. They both knew that nothing was ever as it seemed. The common denominator was the soup kitchen and Tony. But Tony was gone.

After a while, Annabel's tears stopped, and she came out and spoke to the volunteers, explaining we had enough food to last until the first week of the New Year. After that, we would be looking for donations for food again, and they will have to be on the lookout for a new place to move the Lost Soul Soup kitchen. Their lease will be up in the spring, and the owner has asked them to vacate as the building will be sold.

The soup kitchen closed down for the night. Adam walked Joan and her two kids back to her little apartment. Joan asked Adam if he would like to come in for coffee.

Adam replied, "Yes, if it's not too much trouble."

Joan got the kids to bed. They sat and talked while having coffee about everything and anything. Then Adam realized it was very late; it was time for him to leave. As Adam was leaving, he said it would be a busy day tomorrow, the day before Christmas Eve. It's time to do the Christmas Eve dry run and ensure everything is in order. "Goodnight, will I see you tomorrow?"

"Yes, you will."

58

As Tony left the soup kitchen and walked down
the street, he glanced over his shoulder. He
noticed the two stars following him since the
morning he signed the papers were losing their
luster. Absolutely fantastic, Tony thought. Tony
arrived at the hotel, showered, and went to bed; a
restless sleep followed, and thoughts and dreams
rocked his brain. His parents were telling him to
do the right thing in his dreams. They were there,
and he thought he could touch them; this went on
all night, and finally, morning came. Up he got
dressed, ready for the new adventure to begin.
Grabbed his suitcases and headed down to the
front desk. Asked the agent at the front desk to
put his work suitcase into storage until the end of
January, and he would pick it up. Paid his hotel
bill, got a cab, and headed to the airport. It was
early morning; daylight would not come for at
least three hours. Looked up over his shoulder as
he climbed into the cab; the stars were gone. A
smile crossed his face as he headed to the airport;
he was in the air before long, and all the worrying
was behind him.

He thought his hotel bill was a bit high; as he
looked at the bill, Tony noticed there were extra
charges on his account. Paying for three
additional nights, tonight, Christmas Eve, and
Christmas Day, checking out on Boxing Day was
very strange. He wanted out so fast that he did

not even check the bill. Before long, flying high with angels, Tony fell asleep. Dreams rocked his brain once again. One of the dreams was telling him to forget about Christmas, forget about those people in the church basement. Just get on with your own life; you're not their savior. At the same time, his mother and father were there telling him to do what was right. It's Christmas, Antonio. Help those people. It's the birth of hope, kindness, and love.

In the dream, Tony wondered what would happen to Joan and her kids, Adam, Annabel, and her flock. He could see it all in his dreams. First, Joan was lost without help, the scourge of being alone knocking on her door and depression setting in again, homeless, the kids nowhere to be found. Then, Adam's spirit broke, begging for a beer. Next, Annabel and her flock followed her, looking for whatever scraps they could find. Then his mother and father told him we taught you better. Be humble and kind. He looked out the window. The sun was shining. In a few more hours, the flight will be over. They were descending out of the sky, getting ready to land. The ground was green, and the water was the color of turquoise. Looking into the sky, the two stars were dull, with no life. Even the sunlight could not make them look bright. Tony thought maybe my parents were trying to guide me towards something that would lift my spirits to a new high, but he had left the shining stars behind.

59

They landed, and Tony thought I know what I have to do. I was wrong. I've been given a gift, and it's time to share. He exited the plane, retrieved his luggage, and went through customs. Now, what to do. He had to get back to Thundering Waters. Tony looked at his watch late afternoon. Will he be able to get a ticket and return in time? He approached an agent's desk, "Can you tell me when the next flight back to Thundering Waters is.

The agent looked up, "in five hours."

"Are there any seats available?"

"No, nothing till next week."

"Can you check again for me, please?"

"No, nothing is coming up right now. Check back in an hour if you like."

Tony commented, "I will be back in a bit. I will go over to that restaurant and have a bite to eat. If something comes up, please find me."

Tony went to the restaurant and ordered a meal. Thought to himself, Well, Mom and Dad, if you are the stars following me, I need your help to get back to Thundering Waters. I was wrong. Tony finished his meal and thought maybe it was not meant to be. He walked back to the agent's desk. "Any luck."

"No, replied the agent, that direct flight is booked, and others are ahead of you for a seat. You realize it's December 23, and everyone is trying to get home for Christmas."

"Can you please check for anything?"

"Give me a few moments." The agent called Tony from where he was sitting in half an hour. "I have found something, but I'm unsure if you will be interested."

Tony asked, "What have you found."

"Well, this gets you back to Thundering Waters, but not until tomorrow, Christmas Eve, at one o'clock in the afternoon. It leaves here at midnight and has multiple stops but gets you there before Christmas."

Tony thought for a moment, "Please book it." After several years, Tony felt like he was finding his way.

Tony spent hours in the airport wandering, planning, and waiting until he could get on the plane. Then, finally, he decided he had better make a call to Eric and tell him to hold up on some of the plans they had discussed.

Tony made the call. "Eric, it's Tony here. Have you completed the paperwork to cancel the Lost Souls Kitchen Lease yet?"

"No, I was just going to work on it and bring it to Annabel tomorrow when I do my duty in the kitchen."

"Okay, great, there has been a change in plans. The lease will not be canceled. I'm returning and will see you at three o'clock tomorrow. Please do not tell anyone I'm coming back."

After spending what seemed to be an eternity, Tony finally boarded his flight. He would be back in Thundering Waters on Christmas Eve, with enough time to check in to his hotel, see Eric, and head to the soup kitchen before it opened. The plane took off, and Tony looked out the window as they climbed into the dark sky. The two stars shone bright, welcoming him on his journey home.

After what seemed like an eternity, finally, they landed in Thundering Waters. Tony returned to the hotel. Your room is ready, sir. We knew you would be back. Tony looked at the receptionist. Can I extend my stay for another two weeks? By all means, the receptionist said.

Tony dropped off his bag and had enough time to make it to Eric's office for a quick chat.

Eric was waiting for him, "well, my friend, what happened."

"I don't know. What I realized was that I was given a gift. The plans I developed to drop everything are not what my parents taught me to do. I knew it was wrong, and I'm glad I returned to do the right thing. These people need some help and guidance. We won't issue that check to Adam just yet; I will do it myself. Regarding the Lost Souls Soup Kitchen, we will set up a trust fund for them and offer the church basement on a long-term deal at no cost. The Church will not be sold. I will make Thundering Waters the headquarters for my company." Tony looked at Eric, "I think it's time we head over to the kitchen."

"By all means, let's go. I think this is going to be a Christmas Eve everyone is going to remember."

They made it to the kitchen just as Annabel spoke, giving her troupe of volunteers words of encouragement. We had a terrific run last night, with not too many glitches. We will try and do the same thing tonight. I suspect we will have a lot of lost souls this evening. She told everyone that God would watch over them no matter what happened tonight.

"Excuse me," Annabel heard a familiar voice. She looked over to the doorway, Tony standing there looking somewhat disheveled.

"What would you like, sir."

"I thought you could use an extra hand."

"Are you a worker or a lost soul looking for a meal?"

"Both, but I want to say something before you open the doors."

Annabel looked at him and thought, God is working again in mysterious ways. "By all means, please come forward," she said.

"I came across the soup kitchen a few weeks ago while walking around town. Something drew me to this location. I don't know what it was, but there were a couple stars that I could see that seemed to be my guiding light.

"The other night, I told Annabel she would have to be out in the spring. The renovations would be completed by the end of March, and the building would be sold. When I first saw this building, something told me I had to buy it. Why, I did not know. This building had no fond memories for me. Years ago, just outside on the corner, my parents died in a horrific car crash on Christmas Eve, so I'm not fond of Christmas or my birthday. Both days just bring memories of a sad time in my life. However, these past two weeks after meeting everyone in this room has lifted my spirits, reignited my feeling for life, and brought new hope for this time of the year.

So, with this news, the renovations will continue in the New Year. The Eagle Mining and Prospecting Corporation will relocate to the upper floor of the old church. At the same time, Lost Souls Soup Kitchen will take up permanent residence in the basement of this beautiful building. It will be a place where we will offer warmth, food, and work when available to our patrons, the lost souls. We will endeavor to help when and wherever we can. My other new company, Black Wolf Reality, will be charged with locating sustainable housing for our patrons who need a helping hand.

I am making four offers to individuals I feel can help get this project off the ground. These individuals have no idea what is happening. After these announcements, they will have time to decline the offers. The Lost Souls Soup Kitchen and the Black Wolf Reality company will be subsidiary companies under The Eagle Mining and Prospecting Corporation. I'm hoping that Ms. Annabel Heaven will run the charity. Her office will be on the main floor, where she can do God's work regularly. I also want to offer Adam Watson the position of CEO and President of the Eagle Mining and Prospecting Company. With all this happening, I would be remiss in not having someone take care of the finances. At this time, I would like to offer Joan Rivera the position of Chief Financial Officer for our new endeavor.

Last but not least, with us taking on the task of sustainable housing, I would like to offer Mitch Brown the position of Vice President of Construction. This will be a dual role, helping Black Wolf Reality and Adam Watson with camp setups on our mining side. I don't expect answers from you right now. The New Year will be fine. I will be traveling and trying to find the next star for the company.

Now, I will turn over the proceedings back to Annabel."

Annabel looked over, looked up to the heavens, and thought, with tears streaming down her face, thank you, lord. She didn't care if Tony saw her crying at all. She looked at her husband, Harry, open the door. We have a lot of hungry souls to feed tonight.

Eric, Giuseppe, and Angelina were smiling. Giuseppe leaned over and whispered in Angelina's ear. I knew there was dark magic among us. Annabel saw Giuseppe whispering to Angelina. She looked over at Giuseppe and winked. Giuseppe slowly moved behind Angelina so Annabel could not see him. He was having none of her Black Magic. Annabel thought to herself the good lord indeed works in mysterious ways. She prayed for a benefactor, and a lost soul walked through her door only to become the benefactor she prayed for.

Epilog

In the New Year, Tony's friends accepted his offered positions. The company and the charity would grow strong under the watchful eyes of the new guard running the show from the home base. Joan and Adam became a couple and married a year later. Adam accepted Johnny and Lucey as his own. Annabel thanked the lord every day for the beautiful miracle she received. Mitch continued locating and setting up sustainable housing for the lost souls. She also found a way to incorporate the steeple into the redesign of the old church. Two lights shone into the night sky like stars reaching the heavens. This became a beacon of hope for those seeking a hot meal and a warm place to converse. Now, Tony was not the only one that could see the light. Christmas and his birthday now reminded him of the good in the world. He helped where he could and continued to find new stars for the company. As far as Tony's stars that followed him through this journey, they shone their brightest that night and disappeared, except they were always in Tony's heart.

Manufactured by Amazon.ca
Bolton, ON